For Gordon
Diann,
who play well
rain or shine...

The Shakers
Play Better in
the Rain

Saltville and the
Ten Commandments

by Stan McCready

Stan McCready

'93

Companion Press
P.O. Box 310
Shippensburg, PA 17257-0310

"Good Stewards of the
Manifold Grace of God"

ISBN 1-56043-527-5

For Worldwide Distribution
Printed in the U.S.A.

Dedication

Darden "Smile" Towe
1936 - 1992

In many fields timing is everything. In searching for the right Saltville family or McCready family person for this book's dedication none would come up uniquely fitting.

During the last week possible (because of deadlines) my longest standing friend, Don W. Smith, who hardly knew but liked an Emory and Henry graduate, phoned to say Darden Towe was dead at 56. I knew then the proper person, the dedication must go to the one non-family, non-Saltville person who best illustrates the content and intent of this book.

I first saw this speedy bulk, not hulk, win a Fulterton Field foot race, unbelievably. My first contact with him was a blue and white "Smile" card. His constant characteristics of humor, caring, helping, hoping and a hallow respect for all levels of campus life from black, one armed Charlie Foster to President Earl G. Hunt, Jr. embodied his Shaker-Christian concept to a provable, usable reality.

Weird as it sounds now, I asked him to serve in the student government president's cabinet along side the stock positions. His being caused me to create the post Secretary of "School Spirit."

One odd example of his fervor and grace occurred one of those gray, fall Emory Monday afternoons when our football team had lost a bad one on Saturday.

Darden with picket in hand —"Go Wasps"—looking like the Pied Piper, began at the far end of the wet, leaf laden campus and gathered a motley crew of male, female, fraternity, non-fraternity, jock, non-jock, younger and older students from dorm to library and burst onto the practice field with a banner beaming smile and a spontaneous rendition of the school fight song:

> Across the hills of ole Virginia there comes a melody divine. It fills our hearts with eager longing and sweetest melody divine. It fills our hearts with eager longings and friends we love so dear. So now we're singing voices ringing love we bringing you. Rah! Rah! Rah!
> Hail Emory, hail Emory, hail blue and gold true as of old hail Emory, hail Emory, hail to ole E.H.C.

So Darden, the 10 miles from Fullerton Field and Memorial Chapel to Shaker Stadium and Madam Russell Church were never closer than in your being. May God grant you the eternal peace in heaven you so sowed in Virginia at Emory, and Saltville.

Holy cow, how strange Secretary of School Spirit sounds now but he pulled it off even as a leader in the opposition campus political party!

So to the immortal spirit of Darden "Smile" Towe I give thanks for his blessing of true greatness for he best showed over four decades even at a distance the

Shaker/Christian spirit as the Good Book says, "He was without guile."

The Shakers and the Wasps play better in the rain.

Darden Towe and The Jefferson Award

A Page of Appreciation

While dedication of a work might more logically go family or friend appreciation seems more futuristic and so is the Spirit of God in places and people, I enter this special page and picture.

The role these four families, from three different generations, play in this person's life and faith defy my capacities to express. Even this comedy caper catches only in part the blessing of the four women in my life's picture. The Andy Griffin coined phrase gets at it only partly. "I *appreciate* you, ladies."

McCready Family Christmas Picture 1990:
left to right, front row: **Jean, Ruth.** Back row: **Carla,
"Frisky", Judy and Stan** (photo by Ron Kirk).

Contents

Comments

Stan's clever ability to describe these incredible people and this very unique town plus the meat of the spiritual message he delivers made Lois and me laugh, cry and celebrate–it is fantastic.

Football Coach Harry Fry (retired)
Gate City and Saltville High Schools

Some gifted clergy effectively record their refreshing insights, ideas and experiences. Stan McCready in this his first book demonstrates this gift with arresting perception, skill and grace.

H. Ellis Finger
Bishop, United Methodist Church (retired)
Knoxville, TN

Stan has done a marvelously interesting and thought-provoking book showing the relevance of the Ten Commandments to life in a community. That he'd rather be viewed "as irreverent than irrelevant" makes me glad.

Dalton Roberts
Hamilton County Executive
Chattanooga, TN

Stan McCready was my student and is now an effective Christian minister gifted with unique skills in communication. This surprisingly candid volume is a fascinating piece of vintage Americana featuring a colorful little industrial town in Southwest Virginia, and using it as background for a refreshingly different, often earthy, contemporary study of the Ten Commandments.

Bishop Earl G. Hunt, Jr
Former Emory and Henry College President
Retired United Methodist Bishop
Lake Junaluska, N.C.

Refreshing! Brings the Ten Commandments home to the young searching reader.

David Bradley
Senior Journalism Student
University of Tennesee

This collection of stories using the Ten Commandments as a gathering tool warm our hearts, strike a note of humor, and give us insight into a generation past while lifting up Christian values. I will admit that just as some of Stan's sermon titles made me "raise an eyebrow" so do some parts of this book. I'm sure that both the language and the seventh chapter are true to life, and Stan's ever-present sense of honesty dictated to him that those things be a part of his strangely heart warmed memories of the special place, Saltville.

Jean Henderson
Author, Organist, Grandmother and former
Holston Conference Lay Leader

This book is a reaffirmation of the basic goodness of small town communities, characterized by strong family ties, loyalty and pride. Throughout its context of the Ten Commandments is interwoven the healthy humanness of essentially good people who sometime stray from the straight and narrow.

Through it all Stan's zest for life, loving disposition and sense of humor are fresh breezes in a world which seems far more focused on the ills of a complex civilization.

I treasure my copy and expect to refer to it frequently. No resident of Saltville or Southwest Virginia should be without one, and even those who never heard of Saltville will enjoy a return to a more gracious era.

William C. Wampler, Sr.
Former Congressman

Foreword

I first met Stan McCready more than a few years ago when he was serving as a Communications Specialist for Holston Conference, of the United Methodist Church. I knew right away that he had an unusual but effective way of "communicating" whether it was the spoken word or the written word. He had a way of catching your attention without using the old rule of communication that says one has to hear something at least three times before one remembers.

Years later when he became my pastor I was amazed (and sometimes appalled) at some of the sermon titles he would use. It was not uncommon to read what the message would be on a particular Sunday and wonder how in the world he would get any spiritual truths for us from such a title. Somehow, he always did bring a relevant and meaningful message that did indeed challenge us to deeper spiritual thinking and doing. And it was that unusual and creative way of communicating that was uniquely his that caused us to remember what might have been otherwise forgotten by the time we had driven from the Sanctuary of the church to the sanctuary of our home.

Stan has given us a sampling of his unique style of communicating in this book. I've never been to Saltville but I feel "akin" to many of its residents who come alive in this book. Saltville was not unlike the little Southwest Virginia town of Jonesville where I spent a lot of my youth so I could relate to many of the scenes and situations he "paints with words."

This collection of stories using the Ten Commandments as a gathering tool warms our hearts, strikes a note of humor, and gives insight into a generation past while lifting up Christian values. I will admit that just as some of Stan's sermon titles made me "raise an eyebrow" so do some parts of this book. Some readers may feel uncomfortable as I do with his inclusion of the irreverent language used by some of the characters and some may feel uncomfortable as I did when I read the chapter on the seventh commandment. I'm sure that both language and the chapter I referred to are true to life, like it or not, and Stan's ever-present sense of honesty dictated to him that those things be a part of his writing.

I once read an evaluation of the great preacher/professor Albert Outler. The statement went something like this: "Outler is a preacher with a style all his own, a theologian who doesn't sound like one, a theologian who refuses to talk down (or up) to his audience. And yet one who manages to communicate to thoughtful people, hold their attention with what some would call heavy stuff, and leave them turned on to the grace of God."

That description aptly fits my friend, Stan McCready. in *The Shakers Play Better in the Rain* he speaks from a heart warmed by the memories of the people and places of his home town and warmed "strangely" by the same spirit revealed to us who stand in need of hope and healing.

Jean Henderson

Mrs. Jim (Jean) Henderson was the first female lay leader of Holston Annual Conference of the United Methodist Church; led the election of laity delegates of General Conference twice; chaired the Conference Communication Commission; a member and organist of Wesley Memorial United Methodist Church, Cleveland, Tennessee for 32 years.

Jean is the only child of The Rev. Ogleva and Marie Street. Jim and she have two sons and three grandsons.

She authored *Leaning on the Promises*, a statement of faith after the 1977 accidental death of their middle son who was in preparation for ordained ministry. She is an accomplished public speaker.

This author and his family have been blessed through her family's ministry for over a fourth of a century.

Gabriel's Last Blast
An Introduction

Welcome to a real Wobegon—the Lake Wobegon created for National Public Radio by Garrison Keillor. Garrison's lake as well as his ladies, men and children is fictional.

Welcome to Saltville, where all the children, men, and women are, if not handsome, at least very real. The string of stories which follow are listed in the categories of the Ten Commandments which Moses delivered from Mt. Sinai handed him by the good Lord (as God was affectionately called in Saltville). We had not Sinai but we did have Lover's Leap on the south and Red Rock Mountain on the north coupled with Rich Valley on our east and Poor Valley on our west: two mounts and two valleys which graced us geographically. To many this area was our promised land. While there was some honey and plenty of milk flowing, we eventually balanced the farm richness of incredibly black loamy soil with the deeper earthen treasures of massive salt and limestone deposits from the Old and New Quarries, the ever present gypsum from Plasterco on the west and North Holston on the east, and nearby king coal.

We lacked only oil but so did the Israelites since the Arabs ended up with all of that blessing/curse.

Saltville is a real place and in many real ways a promised land.

Roy Maiden, the massive mover of furniture for Charlie Wiley, was more trusting in government to change society than in the church in his early years. But even as a young man, "Stife's" fervent belief in Saltville and God showed through when he loudly declared, "I firmly believe that when Gabriel blows his horn, he'll be standing on Lover's Leap in Saltville, Virginia."

As one who was bred, born and reared in Saltville, I have wanted to capture some of its reality for posterity and myself. Some say each of us has one good book and one good sermon in us. I hope this is that book for me and I pray that I have more than one good sermon since I am an every Sunday preacher.

This writing has taken five years through thick and thin. Most of it if from personal recall. Many and various helps have come from too many to name lest I leave many more helpful folks' contributions unnamed.

Somewhere the phrase has come from my gestation or memory, I do not know which; "In Saltville everybody knows your name and everybody seems to be the same." Having preached and spoken in many of the great states of America, I found myself using many Saltville stories as homey but relevant illustrations. One story stands foremost in my sharing.

Sometimes relatives question the accuracy of the names and numbers in the story but if the totals and names are off somewhat, trust this preacher that it is a truly true Saltville story.

Perhaps the same will be said about other stories in this writing, and all I can say is I am sorry in advance to be in error or to hurt any feelings. But the reports are as I remember them or as shared by others. No one gets picked on more regularly or cast in the bad light more thoroughly than this deserving author and his family.

Prepublication reviews ran complimentary though some were anxious about my hurting folk mentioned and their posterity. When I could check with the folk directly, none reported foul.

The beware of hurting others always came from relatives and friends. Thus I have adjusted reports with directness and names and hope the reduced directness does not dilute the personalized message of these very folk whose stories rallied my hope.

Responding to concerns of language and content, I guess this is a "P.G." book but not nearly as graphic as II Kings 18:27 (King James version) in four letter words or as violent or sexual as Genesis and the Song of Solomon.

As always with risk from my first sermon against segregation to my last editorial in Holston United Methodist (a pro and con writing on Bishop Scott Allen's departure), I would rather be considered irreverent than irrelevant.

The best Saltville story illustrates much about our town, and you who know the town can see the many applications. For you who do not know our town, come up or down and see us sometime. There really is a "Lake Saltville."

My favorite Saltville story began in the late 1920's depression when there was little money or entertainment in Smyth County, Virginia. But the Rich Valley Fair and Horse Show kept its annual date. Bass Smith who fathered 24 children by two wives (the first one died after 12 children) is the main contributor.

There were so many Smiths around the house that a poem for roll call developed. Some of it, according to Ed Cahill, went:

Alf, Cal, Hobe, Pres
Albert, Leonard, Oat and Chess

Mary, Kate, Gert, Feen
Kansas, Texas, Mac and Rene

Fount, Bertie, Nannie, and Doane
And if you don't believe me,
I'll take you to my home!

During the fall matinee of the Rich Valley Fair, the farm man Smith wanted to see a Brahma bull on display. With his clan in tow, he approached the box office only to turn away disappointed. It was a dime a head and too costly for the daddy and 21 kids present in that depression era. The out-of-town ticket salesman was curious about Bass and his following, so he asked, "Hey, mister, are all those kids yours?" Bass returned and answered proudly, "Yes sir, and I have three more at home." The amazed ticket barker yielded saying, "Come on in free. And bring all those kids. I want the bull to see you all."

One of the usual responses is that this story is full of bull and of course presumed not true. But 'tis as so as Saltville is real.

The pages of this story are limited almost entirely to the period of my remembrance from 1945 to 1965. Stories beyond Saltville from neighboring towns and Emory and Henry where I spent heavy time as a student and later pastor are painfully excluded in order to hold to one period and one place. The notion for this book came when I did a series of broadcast and published sermons at First Centenary United Methodist Church in Chattanooga, Tennessee. I noticed how I often used Saltville illustrations, and when people pushed me toward publishing, the concept of a working title came, *Saltville and the Ten Commandments*. Since some of the best Saltville stories cannot be twisted even by this preacher into any one of the chapters on the ten commandments, I chose to close with a catch-all chapter.

I have chosen to make as positive as possible this presentation. The names have not been changed but left out to protect the guilty. Anyone hurt by any story is given my fullest apology and personal sorrow. Let me know so I can know and respond.

My purpose is to show how a place and a people tied to the real God can enrich all of life. Our town was particularly religious with many churches and certain high moral standards, but we also had our odd logics and blind sides—segregation being one for us and our southland. A strange one was shared by Dr. Albert Bowles when he served three United Methodist churches surrounding the Saltville hills and basin.

A well-known motel was renting a room weekly to a group of men who met one night a week for illegal gambling. The "game" as it was commonly known became the focus of the Saltville Ministerial Association. The ministers sent representatives to confront the owner who did not deny the gambling. His justification was that he did not keep the rent money but gave it to a different Saltville church every Sunday.

Such presence of faith and practice of odd logic caused this eight of nine children to long ponder a field of service.

The death of Dad July 17, 1944, was more pivotal to my life and that of our entire family than we could see then. Even the good Dr. Soyars who lived two houses below left our home that fateful morning after seeing Dad dead from a heart attack without a word to Mom or us. He just pulled the sheet over Wyndham McCready and called Rybe Henderson.

I took long, lonely walks during the years from age seven through high school—often wondering what to do in life and sometimes wondering what life was all about. Twice I considered life not worth the hassle, but having done suicide funerals I knew I did not want one of them for myself or mine. One place became the most meaningful for walking, self talking, and God talking with a purview for life's preview. The "mound" southeast of the high school and north of McKee Hospital—a tree laden hill we called Lover's Leap—was my best point for spiritual reference. This was the same spot Roy Maiden, I later learned, tabbed as Gabriel's point for the announcement of Christ's return.

From there I could see a baseball diamond and outfield. Figuratively I saw one corner of the diamond as my school, another the town hall, a third our church, and home plate was our large frame house at 114 Easy Street. Following the baseball diamond map, I could "see" the hospital, golf course, ball field, Mathieson Alkali Works, and the last point of focus was the town businesses. Those nine positions, like a baseball field, became in effect my "places of the heart" or "field of dreams." (To borrow and play on two great movie titles.)

What shall I do for a lifetime? Where? When? How?—Ah, the old "W" questions. I was a tall, thin, awkward, acne scarred kid who changed from a scared first grader and good student to a bully and disinterested student by grade eight. The interaction in athletics, politics, and the Christian church created my most natural line for a career. After breaking a collar bone in football and reaching no further regular baseball play for the Shakers than third base coach, I decided against pursuing sports for a career in favor of eating regularly. A couple of student body officer wins and losses at Emory and Henry College along with an almost addicted sociological interest (would not have known it by that name then) I settled in on law and politics as a likely career. Despite a couple of excellent law school scholarships and persistent confrontation with the gods of all nine positions from the Lover's Leap Map, I accepted the call to preach (minister) in August 1960 while in meditation on the peak of Saltville's Lover's Leap. So to Roy "Big Stife" Maiden I say I reckon I heard some of Gabriel's pre-trumpet call. That acceptance has still allowed me to minister in various communities and often in all nine of the previously mentioned areas.

I had a dream, a vision for our world, and hoped for some helpful role in it. But there was also a nightmare, or more often, a recurring bad dream in my life with my awakening to recall being in front of a large crowd scheduled to deliver a significant message and I was totally unprepared. My first sermon in August 1960, in Saltville was "Be Prepared," a play on the Scout motto.

That haunting dream couples with the strange story I back filed, thinking it would not fit or help this book. It seems a Shaker junior varsity team (most uncharacteristic in the 1950s) found itself with a scoreboard halftime deficit of 40 to 0. At halftime the angry coach and beat up players came to "reason together" for the second half. Don "Guinea" Price, the best runner, declined when they suggested he run the ball more. "I'm beat to death already," said "Guinea." The defense got defensive when the coach suggested they rush more. Mac Campbell said, "Coach, they've got us outweighed 30 pounds per man. Let's call off the second half." Then G.R. "Nyoka" Cannon, not noted for his speaking up, suggested a strategy that was unique. "Boys, when we get the ball, let's just have Willis (Jerry) throw some short incomplete passes. That way, it will look like we're trying and nobody will get hurt."

What a commentary on too many of us today. Let's go through the motion of living (playing) but don't really try to win. Holy Cow!

But thanks be to a holy God and a near holy and real people and real place called Saltville. For me and many: You were/are the salt of the earth.

To be the salt of the earth requires the container of distribution. Perhaps that is what Jude Call had in mind when he won the contest for naming the Saltville High School newspaper—the "Salt Shaker". Later appropriately, the Saltville Maroons appropriated the term and became the Saltville Shakers.

Such an unique and relevant name caught a Paul Harvey's news cast when the school merged and gave up the nick name in 1987.

The book title seems a natural for a book about a town's faith and determination.

On the streets of Saltville and in the hallways of home and school, a chant of confidence and truth rang out on cloudy Friday afternoons. When asked our chances in the big football game that Friday night, we all knew it was more than right when young and old would nearly sing, "the Shakers play better in the rain".

Chapter 1

Closed for the Funeral

Saltville, like most of us, violates the first commandment concerning idolatry easier than any of the "big ten." We would say the first big commandment was our least violated one standing along side the commandment about killing folk.

Our idol worship in the 1940s, '50s and '60s compares the old native totem pole of the Indians to the current goal of the boys with the most toys. From the prehistoric dinosaurs licking salt on the Saltville shores for health and spice of life to the Saltville socialites and street strollers grabbing over prescribed legal drugs to stealing Sterno (canned heat) at the local hardware store, we had our own chemical idols; and not all were those Olin or Mathieson Chemical products! The abuse of drugs and the idolatry those abuses create and perpetuate are subtle, gradual and most far reaching. The town, nation, and world may ultimately be lulled under. "Crack," the cheap destructive one, may break our back.

The leading abused drug from Saltville and the world has always been alcohol. The most popular legal forms range from "government liquor" and 3.2 beer to homemade wine from the dandelion to the grape. The illegal form, "white lightning," was made in a variety of stills dotting the mountain ranges.

Even the re-legalization of liquor in the '30s did not stop the stills from smoking regularly despite the revenuers' raids. If chemical abuse can be understood as an idol and illegal or legal drugs can be understood as potential gods, then the seeking Christian has the battle partly begun and won.

The proper use of legal alcohol and prescribed drugs need not be herded off with the other abuses as evil or ungodly. Saltville reacted, as did the nation, in the 1920s and tried to eliminate an overindulgent practice with total prohibition. Some called it a "noble experiment" which failed. The use of alcohol/drugs as a rite of passage (something Saltville youth also did to prove their maturity) has started more folk on the road to drug ruin than any other introduction. Total abstainers can never become alcoholics. That stance has saved me and many Shakers from the ruinous route of alcoholism.

E. Roy "Buck" Arnold, Jr., tells of a group of boys camping out on Tumbling Creek with poor sleeping equipment on a cold and rainy night. A prayer meeting was taking place at the old school/church structure with an inviting roll of smoke coming from the pot bellied stove. As a handful of faithful Wednesday night worshippers sang "Blessed be the tie that binds," the boys, already wet with rain and "wet" within from "moonshine," wandered and waddled in and headed straight for the stove.

Suddenly, "Spot" Heath allowed a "shine bottle" to fall from his coat and hit the floor with a loud thud, but it did not break. The music stopped and the church folks focused on "Spot." With quick recovery, he swiftly stuck the yellowish pint in his pocket and declared, "Mustard, mustard!"

Compared to the restless adventurous experience of youth, most of whom outlive their wanderings, comes the fervent and odd "right of business" assumed peculiarly, at least by one local bootlegger, to sell his wares. In the 1960s many of us youth pointed out our hypocritical laws and the lack of enforcement in several areas. I began a limited but pointed series of letters to our local newspaper editor concerning "the on the sly illegal gambling in a couple of public businesses" and the easy circulation of bootleg liquor from some taxi drivers and private homes.

The most flagrant of the traveling Saltville liquor outlets was a lanky, wild-eyed follow who often wore a black chauffeur's cap and spoke his sentences in an excited staccato type voice. (I'm not sure if he wore the cap to designate the fact that he was a cab driver or to camouflage the fact that he was a bootlegger.) When sales began to slow, the "traveling liquor entrepreneur" had had enough. He dressed me down saying, "Listen here, you meddlesome preacher, I fought four years in the islands all over the Pacific for my rights in WWII. I earned my rights and nobody is taking them from me. I've got my rights like everybody else to make a living by selling liquor. I've got children to support..."

I decided not to debate a fellow who confused service in the military to uphold international law as earning the right to resell alcohol, always a violation of local laws.

Some say this "traveling liquor entrepreneur" placed a sign on his taxi during the funeral of Saltville icon R.B. Worthy. The sign read, "Closed for business during the funeral."

My letters continued and his complaining increased, which probably illustrated, on both our parts, the absence of wisdom and the intensity of emotion always related to the drug and alcohol issue.

Saltville had an intense increase in that abuse led by (1) the hunger and thirst after excitement, (2) the need to escape reality, (3) the need to rebel, (4) the high degree of boredom in a high-tech society coupled with the time of the general advent of broad drug use in America, and (5) the Olin plant closing and all of its related problems.

The massive mood of insecurity and practical panic caused Saltville to move rather thoroughly into the new drug era from "old barley corn" to the new levels of chemical experimentation and dependence.

The list of alcoholics and drug addicts is both too long and improper to appear in this print. Some of my best friends and relatives would head it. Two names can be risked since they came from my family, the McCready and Debusk clans. These concrete symbols, which the reader can use to create his or her own personal examples, perhaps will speak for us. Hardly a family of any size can claim a drink- or drug-free family tree. One of our early drug addicts was Aunt Mabel McCready who befriended a male who had direct access to legal drugs and she became a problem in the 1930s, long before drug addiction became common. I buried her in 1974 from a nursing home still carrying the tragedy of her early sad choices.

An uncle on the Debusk side who practiced dentistry and umpired baseball, both with great skill, met an early death at age 51. H.E. Diggs called Jimmy "a great little baseball player and a better dentist drunk than many sober." Dr. James Knox "Jimmy" Debusk was the youngest of ten and the first to die. He was found dead in his dental chair from drinking grain alcohol. His office had declined in size to a single front office room in the old Salt Theatre building.

These family facts serve to admit our problems and admonish friend, foe and stranger. Let's try to hunger and thirst after righteousness—the right way. Positive hunger and thirst help avoid the ever present plague from new Coors to Old Crow to the newest cocaine— crack. These user-friendly chemicals become user-unfriendly permanent plagues.

Developing a point on the subject of Saltville and the danger of communism sounds out of sync with the recent fall of that once powerful persuasion but it still represents the subjects of politics and fear.

Since 1917 the political doctrine of Marx, Lenin, Stalin, Khrushchev, and all the way up to Gorbachev has been well-known in the valley. However, dialectical materialism runs into serious trouble in the Mathieson/Olin Valley era. The plant began in 1892 about the time the Czars were wearing out their welcome by neglect and abuse of the Russian masses.

The political philosophy of any area grows out of its economic, religious, psychological and sociological traditions. Represented by the individualistic nature of Patrick Henry's sister, Madam Russell, of the Revolutionary era, to the anti-slavery sentiments of Southwest Virginia and East Tennessee, we did not have a growing place for even socialism, much less communism.

These areas were too occupied by the mountaineer Scotch Irish and too poor to need or afford, or want slavery. Thus there has never been much sympathy for socialism or atheism in the Mountain Empire.

The Saltville I knew from 1945 to 1965 was heavy in its allegiance to the United States of America, as was the South, a condition I have always thought strange. Why is it the South tends to be more patriotic than the rest of the nation even though she tried to secede from the union and fought four ferocious years before coming back into the fold.

Saltville veterans were able to spot, if not exaggerate, the weaknesses of our own military allies in WWI and WWII. I remember some veterans on the sidewalks of Saltville calling the British and the Russians worse names than the Japanese and the Germans.

But Saltville's quest for security and meaning made it potential for making America and materialism an idol. While few folk knew Professor Frederick W. Parkhurst, Jr.'s view at a nearby college, the Professor's view would be ascribed to by most. The Emory and Henry Quaker believed "if you divide up all the money in the world evenly today, tomorrow some will be rich and some will be broke." And yet the true Saltville spirit on materialism is hard to chart. In many ways the town was managed strictly by the corporation. Certainly medicine was as close to being socialized as it gets in America.

One hospital containing four doctor's offices combined with a group medical policy lead many of us to think you didn't pay doctors or hospitals until we finally left Saltville.

Corporation critics called Olin's role closer to "big brother" than to rugged individualism, and maybe all that caused some of us not to be so materialistic in our dreams. Affluent housing never caught on in Saltville. The most expensive car dealer was Chrysler, headed by Bill Hayden, and it failed.

Exclusive clothing never exceeded Howard Board-wine's, "the place to go for brands you know." Perhaps Saltville's most unique sociological oddity was the exposing of so many different people to as classless a society as ever occurs in a free culture! We all attended the same school, recreational areas and commercial sections. While some neighborhoods were more expensive than others, I never recall a zoning fight; and friends married across all neighborhood lines without any thought otherwise.

The company store was popular for variety and credit, yet private businesses also easily operated. A classic story of a laid-back noncompetitive atmosphere came from the Mathieson Pharmacy when a little girl, Barbara Blankenbeckler, ordered coke and potato chips to be charged to her daddy. When the clerk, Leroy Waddell, realized the daddy's name was George Blankenbeckler, he said, "Take the durn stuff free, I'm not writing that long name out for a dime."

And while the dominant national idol of materialism is not exempt from any period of Saltville's history, many of us grew up secure and uninterested in amassing fortunes or even getting slightly rich.

The subject of time and calendar had special stages in Saltville. In the plant heyday the work week dominated. The entire town was signaled by morning, noon and 4 p.m. steam whistle blasts. Things got a bit more frequent and musical in 1949 when the Town Hall clock using Westminister chimes rang on the quarter hour—when the clock worked! While extensive shift work existed, the Monday to Friday day was the routine for most; and except for some Olin executives and merchants, people worked 40 hours and had time for community, church and recreation.

Again the classless society came out in the after-work groupings. Presbyterian and Baptist churches had most of the medical doctors and the shift workers. Methodism, the predominant denomination in the area, was sprinkled with plant executives, merchants, teachers, shift workers, and the masses of women not employed beyond the home.

In recreation, the plant manager's sons played golf with the cab driver's boys. Golf was never known to be the rich person's game. We all swam at the local pool. A disabled laborer's son, the scroungiest, most slandered boy in town, could engage in a good natured water fight with David Bradt, the plant manager's son, and no adults or youth pointed out any real differences.

Segregation was originally enforced from a balcony box at the Salt Theater to a special bleacher at the Saltville Ball Park. Saltville's Black population was less than one percent, and the total of 75 or so Blacks were gainfully employed through traditional janitorial, hospital orderly type roles. A 1922 Mathieson Alkalies publication shows a group picture of 16 male blacks, all employed at the plant.

Most whites respected, if not liked, the even dozen black families of Saltville: the Broadys, Butlers, Clarks, Joneses, Johnsons, Lees, Nickols, Pattersons, Smiths, Soggs, Williams, and Wilsons. But still, high school kids were bussed 72 miles round trip to Bristol to old Douglas High. Hospital orderly, "Doctor Sammy (Cee) Jones," being the most visible of black residents built a brick home on Smoky Row when most white folk were still living in frame houses. Smoky Row, Saltville's segregated housing block, was called "smoky" because of the smoke and cinders from the heavily laden freight trains. The engines bellowed a smoking trail as they pumped up the incline. Some had mistakenly assumed a racial connection with the term "smoky."

While Saltville was more a part of the industrial North with the advent of the Saltville Alkali Works which produced its first product, bicarbonate soda on July 4, 1895, it somehow held much of the slower pace of the former plantation South. Saltville surely had its idols—not only materialism and booze but less obvious ones. Because the near absence of a class culture helped reduce the simple passions of false pride for thousands of Saltville natives and transplants, the experience of idol worship was far less tempting. The near classless society reduced the degree, if not the actual violation, of the first commandment, "You shall have no other gods before me."

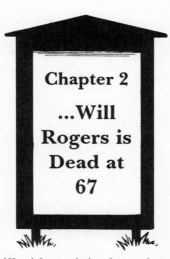

Chapter 2

...Will Rogers is Dead at 67

Idols in Saltville (the original type) started as early as humans inhabited the area. The original folk of the Salt Valley were Cherokee Indians (some Indian racists would consider the Indians savage beasts rather than sacred beings). The many natural gods, which were commonly the sun, moon and stars as well as Indian made totem poles certainly got the white man of the valley interested in idols as gods. If fertility worship could help the white man grow more grain and produce more children for farm labor, then why not try the red man's methods of work and worship. The many archaeological digs, ranging from our home back yard to the 1956 grading of R.B. Worthy High School (Northwood), gave ample evidence of no cowboys here but plenty of Indians and their idols.

The totem pole never penalized Saltville's progress. If anything the Indian's biggest weakness was his multiple gods. When Christianity spread, albeit too often guns came before crosses, the original Saltville settlers were challenged to realign the little gods for the one great "Father who art in Heaven." The happy hunting grounds concept of an always good food supply reveals how basic

11

were the Indians' cultural dreams for a simple existence in Saltville during the 1600s. In the Pioneer period and depression days, basics were no doubt determinative in interest and action. But the richness of soil, abundance of timber, availability of water, and plenty of space (despite mountain ranges) all caused the early "Salt Lick" folk, be they red or white, to have enough basics if not an abundance and to get along well together.

Even the dark 1929 depression hit less severely in Saltville than in other rural industrial towns. Main Street Saltville extends from Smoky Row to McCready's Gap along a four mile stretch of State Highway 91 which once ended as a dirt road in neighboring Tazewell County. Most of the Main Street was residential from Smoky Row to McCready's Gap. All of Saltville's businesses once fronted Main Street, with the original post office and several post-World War II stores starting another business street which extended west to the current town hall.

It stretches the imagination to perceive the small business district as a Madison Avenue, but on those sidewalks and in those stores passed some of the richest and best of God's images and some of the worst graven images.

Saltville's Will Rogers, Kyle Taylor, a cab driver, held forth as the town's greatest sage. From his "position" as a cabbie, Kyle, an arch Democrat, saw much and mused more. Many were the political debates...local, state, and national from cabside to Joe Vernon's barber shop. Kyle once shocked me with a statement which still has me thinking about the complexities of governmental decisions of this day. When I lamented the fact that we needed a man like Lincoln in the White House during Vietnam, his response, introduced by his pet expression which I never figured was irreverent or a vain use of the Deity's name, "Aye God, McCready, let me tell you, Lincoln wouldn't even know how to build a fire in the White House today!" Kyle's clarity of expression was matched only by his distaste for pretense or abstraction. Many years after the Eisenhower-Stevenson campaigns of 1952 and 1956, he confessed that he had voted for the Democrat Adlai Stevenson twice and "I never understood a damn word he said either time."

Long a friendly foe of the Olin Corporation's dominance of business, labor and government of Saltville, he had many pet expressions for local folk too personal to print but highly accurate for the image in which he saw them. He often chided some of his fellow citizens for stealing from their employer, and alleged that he could spot those who were building graven images by simply watching their daily comings and goings. His favorite proof was to point out Mary Spence who continued to walk to work long after most Saltville citizens had progressed enough to own a personal car. "Aye, God, there she goes again...walking to work. Ain't bought a car yet. That proves she's an honest woman. She's not stealing." This was limited logic on Kyle's part, but provocative thought.

Advertising and image making in Saltville were done largely by posters and word of mouth in the '40s and '50s. The first local newspaper, *The Saltville Progress*, began in 1959 and its successor, *The Saltville News Messenger*, continues to this day with a small advertising base. It took until 1982 for Saltville to get a radio station. Most official advertising was limited to the school year book, *The Choo Choo*, and the school paper, *The Saltshaker*. A baseball-shaped sign was hoisted across Main Street to advertise the semi-pro Saltville Alkali's home games; while a car, mounted with a loud speaker from Troy Slate's auction system and accompanied by a background of Well Field frogs in concert, blurted out, "Baseball tonight! The Abingdon Blues versus the Saltville Alkalies at the Saltville Ballpark...8 p.m. ....tickets 50 cents and 25 cents."

Through the benevolent grapevine, Saltville people knew about graven images and whom you could trust.

Not only were images God-like and pagan, but also very little chance existed to distinguish between the image maker and the real thing. Long before it was nationally popular, Kyle Taylor said, "What you see is what you get." He would one day offer the ultimate in political integrity when he won the office of Justice of Peace from an unauthorized write-in campaign. The primary function of the office was to issue warrants for arrests, usually on boozed up men. Kyle resigned the unsought office the next day saying, "Aye God, I ain't taking somebody to the bootlegger in my cab in the morning for money and then writing out a warrant for his arrest that night for more money."

But Saltville's Will Rogers had an early bad image of the church. His long standing reply to revival invitation was, "When you denominations get together, I'll be to see you." I recall, in 1986, being invited as a United Methodist preacher to preach a revival at First Christian Church near Kyle's former home. The year before, Millard "Shine" Taylor, then a Freewill Baptist, had preached and a year later David Roberts, a Nazarene minister, was guest preacher. Kyle had long since died but tears came in the eyes of several of his contemporaries when I recounted the "When you all get together story." On that night alone, once notorious non-church-going folk like Kendall Routh, Roy Maiden, Pete Frye and a once notorious bootlegger were all in respectable attendance! Had Kyle been alive, he too would have been present; for, as the years piled up, Kyle's image of the church had changed from graven to Godly.

When I first entered the ministry in 1960, Kyle said, "Well, I hate to see anybody from two Republican families have to bury me, but you're the only preacher I know who might. Will you?" I agreed on the condition I could check on his spiritual condition from time to time. His emphysema from heavy smoking plagued him worse and worse as he got beyond circulating in the community. One football homecoming visit, I called on Kyle and he could hardly breathe. He had truly accepted Christ and was very repentant not only for his sins but also for the help he could have been to a local church, especially with youth and tough men. Both Kyle and wife Mary died within the next year. I began Kyle's eulogy with, "Saltville's Will Rogers is dead at 67 years of age." There were three ministers of the gospel present, a greatly bereaved family and an overflowing funeral home of old, young, black, white, rich, poor, from all political and sociological categories. Kyle died a real Christian Democrat. And he lived a life with an image which could not stay graven. He exposed, in his many wise words, the graven images and the Godly images of his beloved Saltville.

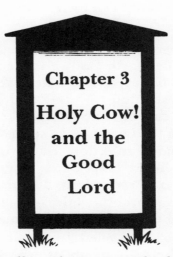

Chapter 3

Holy Cow! and the Good Lord

Saltville, like all southern towns, both glorified God's name and profaned it. Remembering the first time I heard God's name mentioned in Saltville is beyond my recall. Graphic communicators have often contrasted the profane use with the hallowed use of names from the Trinity—the God head, Father, Son and Holy Spirit. Some folk say many children hear God's name more in vain and in slang than in reverence and respect.

We all knew folk who gently mentioned the "Good Lord" in speech and other folk who wickedly ripped out the first person of the God head in special stress situations or in routine banter. Saltville, having the usual verbal hypocrites, heard some fellows and a few gals pray His name on Sunday morning in public and profane His name in selected publics on Monday morning.

A leading member of Madam Russell Church and a long time mayor of the town greatly weakened his witness and had his Sunday school teaching job threatened by his "crossover" language. Some of his Mathieson Well Field crew rebelled saying, "Clean up your Well Field talk or stop teaching our Men's Bible Class."

My brother Rodney, like all six McCready sons, could slander the heavenly Trio by profane declarations. But in a counter declaration I heard him challenge a buddy who had just called forth God's name coupled with the term that holds back rivers of water like Edmondson's Dam. The boy shouted "G– D–" and Rodney asked, "Why don't you call on somebody you know?"

Vain usage of the Lord's name seems universal in appeal but regional in selection. Have you noticed how Southerners rarely use Jesus Christ as a profane expression but Northerners regularly do so? For some odd reason G– D– is southern while J– C– is the northern form of violating the fourth commandment.

No region I have traveled vainly swears by the Holy Spirit, though there are plenty of expressions like holy Moses, holy Toledo, and holy cow. I understand the last word in these phrases though is more apt to be tied to other crude expressions originally than to the Lord.

There are several other ways to misuse God's name than have ever been popularly realized in that southwest tip of Virginia. To take a church membership or marriage vow in God's name and then easily break it is a much more serious "vain" usage of God's name. The religious Quakers and Shakers with special reverence for God's name believed promises should not be made in the Divine's name at all. The founding fathers caught the spirit of that strict religious position between swearing and promising to uphold the Constitution when they, for religious reasons, supplied a second optional word in the presidential oath of office. "I do solemnly swear (or affirm) that I will faithfully execute the office of..." Two Quaker Republicans, Hoover and Nixon, have made the White House.

Saltville voted for Hoover in 1928 and '32 and for Richard Nixon in 1960, '68, and '72.

Many folk have the habit of using either of the first two Deity titles in more a slang than profane way. Kyle

Taylor's "Aye God" and Doctor McKee's "By God" were common to many folk in Smyth and Washington County. Whether the expressions like "dad blame" by Charlie DeBusk or "dad burn" and "dad gum" by many folk were softenings of the other crude, if not profane, terms may send us on a theological rabbit chase or maybe on a course of valid concern. I don't know which. Why folk chose titles from the God head to express simple or complex, anger, joy, frustration or simply to say something, I also do not know.

Our periods of area history and the various stages of individual life and the strictness or looseness of the culture surely are some of the answers.

I remember a fifth grade incident in our classroom in the old white (later gray building) on the west end of the Saltville School Complex. It was the old basement locker room turned into an oddly aligned classroom. Miss Henley Preston was our teacher and the strictest I had in the 20 years of going to schools.

One afternoon she spotted a young boy from Buckeye Hollow reading a funny book during geography class. Henley, or "the witch" we privately called her, quickly moved to the culprit's seat, grabbed the funny book, and ordered him to render his right hand. The closed and raised palm was her well-known fashion for administering paddling, a form of punishment acceptable for boys and girls. With her oak ruler, she regularly administered several sharp raps to many shivering fifth graders. She used very little "due process". Normally, the funny book reader was a quiet, neatly dressed and clean talking eleven year old; but that day, in a wicked and amplified voice, he shouted, "G– D– you, Miss Preston, give me back that book, and I ain't sticking out no damn hand for you to beat on." Even the jock ghosts of Coach

Leonard Mauck and Ray Buchanan were shocked, not to mention the virgin ears of 29 other eleven year olds of the 1949 language vintage.

This was the only time we ever saw the widowed disciplinarian lose control as she stuttered and returned the riled student's funny book. He received it in his left hand, and those nearest him could see his right was drawn and cocked to throw an ink bottle at her in a point blank range. Holy Cow! Maybe a non-religious Shaker demon from the "Old Saltville Maroons" locker room momentarily possessed him.

Years later as a part of the Saltville churches' joint spring revival, we worshippers from seven different churches heard a Church of God preacher dealing with things that destroy our witness.

He moved down the list of commandments saying he could understand why people would lie, steal, commit adultery or even kill...but why would a person enjoy profaning the sacred name of God Almighty or Jesus Christ? I nearly "Amened" him and agreed for years that there was no reason for that sin.

In recent years I am learning that folks who express themselves through forceful vain usage of the Trinity titles may have deep seated religious problems, whether they live in Saltville or Saudi Arabia.

We in the western culture miss the richness of names in general. In the Eastern biblical land's tradition, infants' names were chosen in hopes that the name picked would be a future characteristic. The name itself meant something. Isaac (of Abraham, Isaac and Jacob fame) meant laughter because his mother Sarah laughed at God when she heard his promise that she and Abraham would birth a child in their nineties. Enoch (once Henock) like Enoch Frye, may or may not have been chosen for its original meaning, consecrated. Dedicated teacher Maude Moore reported a black lady (not from Saltville) who, upon attending her first indoor movie, became so attracted to the EXIT sign that she named her first child, "Exit."

For whatever reason, many Saltvillians were given biblical names such as: Noah Smith, Luke Campbell and Luke Colley, Ezekiel Johnson, Isaac Sweat, Joshua Allison, Naomia Swartz, Magdalene Taylor Allison, Nathan Allison, Zenobia McIntyre, Mary Elizabeth Heimann, Moses DeBord and Moses Bunts, and many Rachels (including Rachel Catron).

Also, Saltville had a strong tradition of nicknames which often *did* mean something. E. Roy "Buck" Arnold, Jr., has submitted a list to the *Guinness Book of World Records* seeking to qualify Saltville as the nickname capital of the world. Don Yontz plans a book listing the wide range and long list of Saltville nicknames. The area also has its own version of uniquely named places. Lick Skillet, Pump Log Hollow, Black Dog Hollow, Possum Hollow, Tin Can Alley, Muck Dam, Government Plant, Slaughter Pen Hill, Hill City, Easy Street, Goose Bottom, Smokey Row, N.P. Row, and Thrill Hill are some examples.

Pet sayings, imported as well as homegrown, were common in Shaker Town. Radio brought some, like Jack Benny's "well," which was later practiced by Ronald Reagan. Reagan carried the Saltville precinct in 1980 and '84.

During his 25 years of broadcasting Cardinal baseball, Harry Caray's "holy cow" was heard intermittently (depending on cloud cover) from the St. Louis station KMOX. New York Yankee Network announcer Mel Allen's familiar World Series saying, "How about that?"

crept into may vocabularies as dozens of us gathered around the hardware TV set in the old storeroom of the Mathieson General Store. We heard that expression when Mickey Mantle hit a homerun and we heard that expression when Koufax struck him out.

Until we got our own home TV sets, game after game of each World Series was viewed in the hardware backroom by hundreds. The fact that the reception was poor, snowy, and black and white never seemed a problem for us. "How about that?"

Comparative statements of frustration and discipline would come out as cliches from the laboratory (one microscope only and it was broken) of Margaret Davis. "Why if you did that in the army, you would have to wash 500 windows a day" or "He won't amount to a hill of beans," often echoed from the formaldehyde scented high school laboratory. Perhaps the good Lord could help us all a bit in these days of "anything goes" in dress, language and habits.

What is evil, sinful, bad taste and what ain't (I mean what isn't, Mrs. Eva Ballah) gets to cultural comparisons and personal opinions. John Hammer quoted Luke as reporting Jesus to say, "Let your answer be simply yes or no. Any other comes of evil." Then I recall a lawyer named Sheffield, advising a client named Junior "Scob" Campbell, who was appearing in court after hitting a lady's car while taking me back to Emory and Henry. "Just answer a clear plain 'yes' or 'no.' Any other answer raises questions in the mind of the judge and jury."

I recall hitching a ride with a Smyth County game warden in the late '50s. In the 45-minute ride with the game warden, I raised several questions about county government, hunting and fishing, and all I ever got was a "yes" or "no." I don't know if he was an exaggerated

Jesus incognito or if he was on his way to trial and was practicing the simple "yes" or "no."

At any rate, I don't feel Jesus wants all colorful language of our many languages chopped to a one syllable single word "yes" or "no." To turn the air blue in color and treat the most valuable and precious name in all of history as swear words is not the good Lord's hope for his children.

Perhaps in Saltville "eze" the "by" expression "by Jove" will cap the commandment for us.

Suppose you had two daughters named Jean and Carla. And you would overhear friends and strangers using their names in anger or slang expressions like this. Remember you are over hearing these as the father of these two kids. "By Jean, why don't you get a job and amount to something?" or "By Carla, get the heaven out of here and mow the yard." or "By Jove, he hit that baseball a mile."

Or as James Stewart (the Saltville one) said to Mrs. E.T. Asbury, Sr. (Totie Rector) in her first year of teaching geography and his first time to hear the word Yugoslavia: "Mrs. Asbury, what would a person do if I walked up to them and said, 'You go slavia?'!"

Chapter 4

Joe Dab Goes to the Movies

The use of the Lord's day after World War II changed in Saltville as it did in America but perhaps more slowly because of the conservative religious influence and the power of a corporation operated town.

The Mathieson Alkali Works, later called Olin Mathieson and finally Olin, certainly worked many employees on Sunday. Certain production areas were said to be continuous in nature and demand. The economics of non-stop production created work around the clock and around the calendar.

Corporation councilmen (all men in those days) totally dominated town government and held tight reigns with the support of Virginia's legislated "blue laws." A lack of demand for Sunday shopping saw only drug store items for sale and even then only for a short time of Sunday. The Hardy Roberts Memorial Swimming Pool, Saltville's answer to The Great Salt Lake, was opened between 1 to 5 p.m. along with the Saltville Golf Course. But none considered playing golf or swimming during morning and evening religious services.

One of the most interesting fights between church and state as well as private businesses centered around efforts to have Sunday afternoon and Sunday evening movies in

1954. TV had barely made it over the mountains and that with the help of antenna dotting the horizons with those quaint little ladder type glass insulated wires leading to a few homes. We were happy to get snow cluttered black and white reception coming first from WJHL Johnson City and then from WCYB Bristol.

I remember watching the 1953 Yankee/Dodger Series at the home of Kell Catron with 25 of us crowded into a small living room.

The Salt Theater, owned by a chain with other area theaters, sought to use their capital facilities still another day of the week and to offer Saltville folk the choice of a sixth movie each week. The theater's regular weekly schedule featured a non-western movie on Monday and Tuesday; with a western and a serial episode on Wednesday; and a non-western on Thursday and Friday. The Saturday double feature usually was westerns called "Big Hats" with a second serial series different from the one shown on Wednesday.

Having become a serious church member and having a brother-in-law, Wally Roberts, as the Salt Theater manager, I got to hear both sides of the Sunday movie issue.

The "blue" or Sunday closing laws passed in Richmond had moved from not allowing Sunday openings of most businesses to giving local governing bodies like a town council the option to determine policy. As it had done since the end of Prohibition, the location of local liquor stores was left to the option of the locality. Legislators have a way of dodging the hot issues that we elect them to decide by passing them as hot potatoes back to the voters. Perhaps someday electronic voting will allow all laws to be individually voted upon, and then the legislators' job will go the way of the horse and buggy whip.

This was not so in Saltville in the 1950s. The issue got confused with changes in the law even though the town council and then Mayor J.Q. Peeples solidly voted against Sunday movies.

During the litigation, Roberts reported J.Q. was so mad at him and the Fields Corporation that he promised to have Wally arrested for spitting on the street.

Opinions ran high and many a high school class was diverted into debate on the wisdom and morality of Sunday movies (especially in the Margaret Davis biology classes). The compromise, as Virginia law got more liberal, was that movies might be shown on Sunday afternoon and Sunday night after the churches had finished their evening service (or at least the short winded preachers of the not-so-late meeting churches).

I well remember going to church Sunday night of the first test case. We got out as usual at 8:30 p.m. at Madam Russell Church and headed straight across the railroad tracks to the old Salt Theater. As soon as Wally Roberts saw Joe Dab Moore, Brack Morgan and me settle into our usual front left seats, he signaled "Chicken" Smith to roll the projector.

Just as the lights started down, an uncle of Joe's who was adamantly against the movies tried to wrestle Joe from the theater. The 6'4" gangly basketball center and first baseman was too much for the well-meaning uncle. Joe's line punctuated with angry salvos was, "George, you better get your own boy out of here. "Punior's" hiding up there in the balcony. I've done been to church twice today and he ain't been none and I don't think Doris Day's singing on Sunday night is gonna send me to hell. So turn me loose and get the hell out of my face." Joe's mother, Blanche, had similar words for the would-be Salt Theater kidnapper.

The irony of the church and Olin versus the Salt Theater entertainment on Sunday was that 15 years later, Olin and the Salt Theater closed; and today, many of Saltville's churches continue to hold Sunday evening services.

Among my most pleasant memories of Saltville after World War II was how different Sundays were from the other days, whether you went to church or not.

We lived near the Olin bucket line (tramway), an overhead cable system of one ton bucket-type units which rolled over cable and were drawn by cable nine miles from the New Quarry to the screening plant, visible and audible from our home.

The bucket line never ran on Sunday. All the stores were closed on Sunday except the pharmacy. Schools never did anything on Sunday. I slept on a screened-in back porch during the warm months and always had trouble getting to sleep on Sunday night: there were no clinking sounds from the bucket line tower 120 feet from my bed. Blanche Moore said that church had caused me to get a guilty conscience!

If the Sabbath or Lord's day or any one day out of seven needs to be different for personal, health or religious needs, then Saltville had that special day in the 1950s.

While youth complained there was "nothing to do" in Saltville in general, and especially on Sunday, we grew up to realize there was plenty to do and how good it would be if there were less to do as time passed from the teen years to adult responsibilities.

The one and only universal subject of agreement I have noted in 33 years of ministry centers around the subject of time and activities. All folk after 18 agree that the older we get, the faster time passes. When we were searching for something to do in the 1950s, a week passed the way that a month flies by in latter years. Time is relative to circumstances.

The venerable Mack Poston returned home at 5:30 a.m. after leaving the night before for Saltville Alkali/Marion Cuckoo Burley Belt League Baseball Game. Mack wandered into his house and demanded a big breakfast and a large thermos of black coffee to take to work at the old Ice Plant. Mrs. Poston asked where he had been all night and Mack responded in dead seriousness, "Oh, they tied up and played all night!"

Teachers at old Saltville High and some parents could answer the old "never anything to do" complaint especially at report card time—study more.

Bud Eastridge solved the every six week child/parent confrontation by hiding his report card enroute home in an old Appalachian Power transformer and forging Dave "Come" and Gladys' signature before returning it the next day.

Efforts at organizing teenage recreation were tried by parents like Kay Cahill, but mostly met faltering participation.

High school althletics, skating, golf, swimming and the Salt Theater helped pass our time. "Cruising" began then by walking the beat between the bowling alley, skating rink and Sanders Confectionery or by riding the route of a widening circuit of Chilhowie, Glade, Marion, Bristol and of course Saltville (last call).

We would make the auto circuit as often as our pooled money would allow (gas was only 28 cents a gallon then). The availability of Jimmy Wright's or Billy Blackwell's cars was generally ever present.

Oddly it was 20 years later that a bus load of varied aged folk from Mr. Olivet-Gladeville United Methodist churches in Carroll County helped me see the vast physical and recreational options of Saltville. As the charter bus started its descent on Highway 107, we saw the incredibly level town nestled in the valley backdropped by Red Rock Mountain and framed by the overlook. Bill

Reed asked the question I still haven't answered, "How could you live in this area and not like to hunt and fish?"

In our time, the use of the Lord's day or any day says a bit about us and our understanding of life. The Creator of our spot in the world and the Creator of each of us does care how we care for self, others and the universe. Before we ever heard of the term "fast lane," I was taught and shown by friends, relatives and strangers how rich and full life could be. Things worked then: Study the Good Book from Audrey Hardin's library books; play sports lest you become too bookish; get into one of the many types of Saltville churches lest you become pagan; take part in the political process from theater policy to electing a president (we liked Ike) lest you get cynical; enjoy the good old summer time as first musically intoned from the loud speaker system before the semi-pro baseball game (tunes like Sweet Georgia Brown); help hold up one of the building fronts downtown and learn your first debating skills by hearing Claude Smith try to outpoint Popeye Arnold over a proposed county school consolidation.

A bond issue proposed to build two new Smyth County schools and replace the four older ones: in Brady Bottom, Saltville with Rich Valley; and in Seven Mile Ford, Marion with Chilhowie. The bond issue lost badly in 1951 with only the Saltville precinct voting "yes." We can only wonder what might have been.

I learned a simple lesson, first in Saltville, and then by regional living and international travel: if you have a valid purpose in life, time marches (yea flies) on; and a good break from labor for faith and family strengthens you.

The Mt. Sinai version brought down by Moses to Jesus and to us folk says six days shall you labor but the seventh one is to be out of gear or in the shade (a Saltville shade-tree mechanic translation).

Chapter 5

Shaker Parents did the Best They Could

Mrs. Guy Clear, Mabel, who taught math in the high school and played the organ at Madam Russel Church for 40 years has observed as much religion and education as anyone in town. Though she was not a mother, her comments during a choir practice in 1953 get at parenting as many saw it in Saltville.

Preparing music for the upcoming Mother's Day, the choir, in order to make the music and the sermon compatible, was speculating on the message the Reverend John W. Hammer of Dandridge, Tennessee might preach. Mabel said, "Well, Reverend Hammer's Mother's Day sermons are never very sentimental."

The Reverend Hammer's dominant theme for the fifties was, "There is no juvenile delinquency, just parental delinquency." Parenting in Saltville has changed as has parenting in the nation. But the discernible trend in relation to Moses' directions to juveniles and older children to honor parents brings questions of the town's most honored, our honorable parents. No parent of the year awards occurred then. Naming model parents is hard because the best may never be known. Further problematic is the fact that some kids seem to turn out well regardless of the parents and some kids never get on track regardless of how hard parents have tried.

Just as Jesus sought to spiritually mother a whole city, that same city neglected and crucified him. "O Jerusalem, O Jerusalem, how often would I have gathered you under my wings as a hen gathers her brood and you would not."

Certainly one of Saltville's most faithful and productive families was the Charles Lee Tottens. Bill, George, Chester, K.O. ("Pie") Goldie, Tom and Charles and their families. With the 1927 death of Charles, Mrs. Totten was widowed at 36. Though she rarely ventured beyond the limestone fence of her Easy Street home, her silent but profound mothering sets an example that is one of the bedrocks of motherhood in America. Though sickly most of her life, left with seven children ranging from seven months to 18 years, she labored from the wee hours of pre dawn to late in the evening. Dr. McKee said of Mrs. Maude Totten, "She held that large family together in an outstanding way." Mrs. Totten died at age 96 in 1988.

Another of Saltville's saintly parents would also not be widely seen about town (perhaps that's a part of parenting) but vital to his family now of several generations. His title of Uncle, his longevity (born in 1893) and his faithful leadership at First Christian Church continues to endear Dave Collins to thousands. His children are Everett, Early, Ervin, Mary "Sis" and Evelyn who says, "Daddy was always there when we needed him."

If availability for children makes fathers honorable, then Lawrence "Blackie" Allison wins the award hands down. Since Carlis, Ronnie, Bobby and Roger were in my age range, many were the times that "Blackie" hauled us around and was ever present even after working the hoot owl shift (11 p.m. to 7 a.m.) at the old Ice Plant. "Blackie" would be present for morning baseball games: unshaven, coffee cup in hand and shouting encouragement not only for his sons but for everybody's sons. Love was his motive and athletics has vehicle. So when Abingdom District Superintendent, Thomas Chilcote, preached at Madam Russell Church in 1955 and admonished fathers to spend time with their children, I entered a mental note, "If family time creates Christian points, then "Blackie" breaks the bank in that category."

Family life may have gotten at least one foot down extremely early in Blackie and Ola's marriage. The report is that the couple went to Marion to get married. Enroute home from the Court House, the couple met a bunch of Blackie's baseball buddies who needed a pitcher badly. They asked Blackie to delay his honeymoon and join them to pitch a baseball game. He did!

Another reason why we should honor parents is simply that age is more apt to create wisdom than is youth. Why has America reversed the Eastern tradition of reverencing the aged to worshipping youth? I just cannot understand that one.

One of the many stories associated with the venerable Dr. Thomas K. McKee has the doctor replying after he was asked in his seventies if he would like to be young again, "Hell no, I wouldn't want to be that stupid again for anything."

Claude Smith, long time Mathieson General Store employee, even as a young father illustrated the wisdom of age. Claude took his son, Don, and me on a hiking picnic soon after my Dad's death. We went from their Seven Row home through Elizabeth Cemetery toward the river. In the late forties numerous open sewage streams fed the creeks and the North Fork of the Holston. My lunch bag broke open and a juicy round orange rolled down the bank into the strong gray raw-flowing sewage. Being a frugal Scottish eight year old, I grabbed up my prize dessert and tried to wash it off for salvage and usage. Claude wisely said, "Stan, I don't believe that's safe to try." Often only age can bring the wise answers.

It's hard for me to get beyond my own experience. The number of two-parent homes was very high in that era. But a few of us had the one parent situations more through death than divorce. Like Mrs. Totten, Mother was left with seven children from Don in the Philippines of World War II to Sena as a preschooler. If the unexpected and uninsured death of our Dad, Wyndham Pratt McCready, was not enough for a farm woman of 43 to bear, the couple had already buried W.P., Jr. at age 16 and Mildred at age one-and-a-half. Word came from the Army that Don, 21, had wandered into a Manila military latrine, and had slashed his stomach, wrists and throat. Apparently the "battle fatigue" of a massive and long war, the feeling of family responsibilities as the eldest son, and the location of miles from his Saltville home pushed Don over the brink. Had not a Filipino boy discovered him, the war and the family would have added one more U.S. death to the 292,131 of World War II. Seeing, then in part and now more fully, I wonder how in the world a lady could hold together so effectively five independent and strong boys plus two sensitive and beautiful girls. Five got college educations and the other two opted for early family choices, which are still lasting.

All parents are not honorable and many are the lists in Saltville that failed even the minimal test of accepting and expressing the crucial role of mother and father. Such a list here would be judgmental at best and erroneous at worst. Reality dictates our need to admit that not all of us get honorable parents.

Saltville, like much of world history, has seen parents honor children rather than children honor parents. Parents supported their children in school, sports and music.

The support given students in school, sports and music cause many an example to rush to mind. Perhaps the most rain-drenched football support story goes back to 1957 when hundreds of Saltville fans followed the team to Church Hill, Tennessee. To say three inches of rain fell during that game is not likely an exaggeration. The early season turf and thick Bermuda grass made play possible, though the field was more like a wading pool than a gridiron. Why the game was started or completed remains a mystery but fans and players not only stayed to the end but found it another sweet Shaker victory.

Loyalty to athletics and to youth of the town can partly be realized in the string of perfect attendance at Shaker football games, both home and away, by Herbert "Chub" Arnold from 1942 to 1967 (broken by the Olin strike) and teacher, Don W. Smith, starting in 1958 and currently counting at 357 straight games.

Other than athletic events which draw people from other towns, the event which likely drew the largest crowd was the Kiwanis Club's stunt night. The large number of groups who staged various skits of talent and entertainment always brought out the massive support of youth by parents, grandparents and friends.

I remember particularly Dr. C.C. Hatfield, maybe in a tuxedo, emceeing the program and how Tommy Helton said something that oddly sticks in this mind, "I like the Doc. He's funny."

The only command with a specific reward, "Honor thy father and thy mother so thy days will be long upon the earth" has many meaningful applications to children and parents in the area known as the salt of the earth.

Catching a representative family who honored parents and who had honorable parents drives me around the corner of the old pot holed Easy Street to the first right which is now Second Street. For there lived between the homes of Police Chief Frank Cox and Clint Smith an Olin family most unusual to Saltville nature. Walter, Joanna, Mary, George, and Joe Michael Heimann lived a peculiar life there, having come to Saltville from Elizabethton, Tennessee, as a Nazi Germany refugee family. Walter had lost his job in Elizabethton when the Europeans of his descent were laid off for whatever reasons as war broke out in Europe in the late thirties.

The parents and Walter's mother had seen Hitler's handwriting and had spared themselves who knows what hell or death by coming via the Lady in the Harbor— "Give me your tired..."

Although they were free in the U.S. of A. and although Saltville's Mathieson Chemical Corporation had accepted their passport and given them uninterrupted quality local employment (he was a draftsman), the Heimans took considerable verbal and silent abuse during the war. My dad used to lament over the car pool comments Walter heard daily like, "Them G– D— Germans won another big battle yesterday," or the reverse compliment, "If that Desert Fox Rommel were on our side, we'd beat them damn Germans in a month."

Many Saltvillians, like many Americans, failed to distinguish the vast difference between the Germans who opposed and fled the Third Reich and the Germans who were the Nazis, a single political party that ran Germany into World War II. Dad said Walter never said a word but paid his taxes and bought American War Bonds and designed plans helpful to the U.S. war machine.

A first generation European family from a hostile nation would be one big strike against a family learning to speak English, especially southern Saltville English. But their staunch faithfulness to the Roman Catholic Church when it still used Latin became strike two to many Saltville fundamentalists. The Heimanns drove 50 miles round trip to Marion every Sunday of the year for an 8:30 A.M. mass and staunchly followed their religion despite taunts and argumentative baiting of their family members.

I recall the practice level of application of their faith as the entire Heimann family and I rode around one summer night looking for a drive-in movie that cleared the then Legion of Decency rating produced by the Roman Catholic Church for its members. Not having found the movie on the list, Walter finally said "Well, the priest said if you don't know it's on the list, it's not a sin if you watch the movie." We went. I don't remember the movie, but if it was sinful, I missed the sinful parts during the frequent trips to the popcorn machines.

Originally *Gone with the Wind* was a forbidden movie for the Catholic faith. Perhaps this was due to Scarlet's looseness and to the placement of the Roman Catholic Church in a light role. The Roman Catholic Legion of Decency rating list is now defunct.

Walter, like so many Saltville men, died prematurely in 1960 of heart disease. He, also like many Saltville men, provided well for his family materially. But Walter did not prepare his spouse for his premature exit. Friends, like the Clinton Rapps on N.P. Row, helped decidedly. (N.P. Row, now called Fifth Avenue, was given its original name because in those days a large number of its residents worked in the section of the plant that produced nitrate products.)

The Rapps, according to Mary, were their salvation in decisions since Mrs. Heimann could not drive, write a check, or speak much English. The three kids ranged from elementary to college age. Following the advice of friends, they soon moved to Johnson City to be near East Tennessee State College. All are living and doing O.K., especially when one considers the two big strikes. Mary said recently, "Had we been black we might have struck out!"

Considering the good after-the-war treatment that family, friends and neighbors gave this differently but highly respected, responsible and beloved European family, I believe (in continued baseball parallel) that Saltville, in the long run, helped give the Heimanns a "walk" and they may have hit a "double" themselves.

We learned loads from the Heimanns about the differences in language, religion, race, dress and priorities. Saltville was 98 percent Wasp (White, Anglo-Saxon and Protestant). They learned from us, also.

Mary, who is now a Tennessee Eastman engineer, said of her parents, in an honoring way, something that many a counselor says to folk not sure of how honorable or how honoring they may have been as parents: "My parents did the best they could." Mary, so did most of the parents from Easy Street, N.P. Row and beyond in that dramatic period from 1945 to 1965.

And we folk from far and near to Saltville say "Thanks" to our parents, living and dead. They did the best they knew how.

Chapter 6

Peace in the Valley

My earliest memory of murder takes the form of self murder, suicide, and involves one of our finest families, the Chick Neighbors from N.P. Row. I was preschool age and the idea of self-destruction was very hard for me to imagine. Knowing then and now the other members of that exceptional family made his "checking out" on life even harder to conceive.

The best-known Saltville suicide was surely that of Dr. P.W. Cowherd. This death occurred in 1964 while we were at the New York World's Fair with youth members of our church in Glade Spring, Byars-Cobb. I remember as a rookie minister going to see his mother, a Glade Spring resident. The visit was awkward and probably unhelpful to her as is too often the case with the entire experience of trying to help the indirect suicide victim, the survivor. Why? comes the hard question that too often leads to speculation often far worse than the real reasons. Guilt abounds for family and friends for not spotting the situation in advance and not "doing" anything to avoid it.

Small towns are worse since so many know the person and speculate even more. Suicide would be self-murder whether gradual or all at once. The suicide of a celebrity like that of actress Marilyn Monroe (if it were not murder or an accident) or the type of death Elvis Presley experienced simply fuels the gossip fires and the "inquiring minds" of our lower nature.

Saltville, Virginia, is fortunately located in the Western culture and suicide, unlike in the Eastern culture, is still strongly discouraged. The increased depression and disillusionment from our chemical culture is, however, heading us for a painful increase in the route Judas took when he realized his awful sin of betrayal. I once considered killing myself during the period from April 1960 to May 1962. The thoughts and somewhat serious plans came and went but the better values of the small town, the Western tradition and the Christian prohibition finally corrected those terrible plans.

On to the much more common form of human destruction, murder? —war. Being born in 1938 puts me in that group that church sociologist Lyle Schaller calls pre-World War II, and they are a different breed from the post-World War II generation called "baby boomers".

We sold stamps for war bonds, mashed tin cans and collected milk weed pod for the war effort. Ford and Virginia McKee's sons, Bill and Tommy, greatly influenced and assisted my understanding of the extremely popular war effort in Saltville. From the scary air raid practices within the then Mathieson Plant whistle putting us in the dark of night all over the valley to the dedication of the Hardy Roberts Swimming Pool (Hardy, son of Wyndham, was killed in action in 1942) all made the war very real.

What a joyful day August 15, 1945 was when we were walking the streets of what was popularly called Easy Street and Tommy McKee was shouting as loud as possible from their fast-moving car, "The war is over! The war is over!" The church bells began to ring from one end of the valley to the other and never was there a more popular or exciting after-dark parade in Saltville. I got to carry "Old Glory" and never will I forget that! The quote I remember the most was returning home that night to hear older brother Haynes say, "Russia will be next." Later Korea and Vietnam became household words because of the Russian conflict and in Saltville, which straddles both Smyth and Washington County, we gave up our share of blood, guts, and lives in those far off places.

No military death touched me and folk of my general age more than that of Blake "Tweetie Bird" Farris' military death. He was a namesake of my brother, Blake. "Tweetie" had only a month left in Vietnam when a grenade ended his earthly life. Based on a letter toward the end of his tour there and his usual capacity to wiggle out of troublesome things, I believe he cleared the account with the good Lord. Appropriately, Madam Russell Church is lighted at night by a gift in his memory. At the risk of sounding irreverent to some, I often speak out loud as I pass the cemetery near Glade, "Hi Tweetie, I'm sure everything is all right with you in Heaven and I hope to see you there someday." On a recent snowy December morn, my family paused before Tweetie's name in the black granite of the Vietnam Memorial in our nation's capital.

War is hell according to General W.T. Sherman and is illustrated by buddies from World War II, Korea and Vietnam. From sidewalk stories to deep personal counseling I have learned of the veteran's guilt, hurt, fear and physical damage that goes with war. Thus all scars are not battle scars.

The existing entry sign which reads "Welcome to Saltville, the Salt Capital of the Confederacy" is a proud reminder of the fact that Saltville was the site of two Civil War battles. Saltville, like so many small American towns, has paid her dear price in deaths and scarred veterans as well as reaped the rape of interruption of the "peace in our valley."

On the highly volatile issue of abortion, Saltville, like most small towns, experiences much the same evolution of views and practices as the rest of the south and the nation. To use this adage with this subject may seem too close in parallel but "necessity is the mother of invention." Technology has allowed tremendous advances in reducing the size of family and the need for large families. From Bass Smith's 24 children to many childless marriages, Saltville and the nation bear less children. From the pill to current reactivation of the condom, birth control is common knowledge but apparently still poorly practiced. The number of pregnancies among the 200 girls in the local high school in recent times plus the undetermined number of abortions suggests that passion, poor planning and age-old ignorance are still rampant in Saltville. Men and women, as well as religious and non-religious folk, differ strongly on the right or wrong of abortion. The vast majority support abortion and my favoring of all other forms of birth control except abortion are too colored by my being male, religious and nearly the victim of an abortion.

In November 1937, the oldest of six children, my brother W.P., was stricken with a carbuncle and died suddenly. "The brilliant mind and gentle spirit" as Roy Maiden has described him died quickly in the old hospital above the General Store. Sulphur drugs were not discovered then and what is now a routine infection was then an experience of his literally turning green with infection and dying. Only weeks later, Dr. R.D. Campbell determined my mother's pregnancy and suggested abortion because of mother's emotional state and the already large family. He told mother I would likely not be healthy physically or mentally. She thought about it for only a few minutes and obviously refused. Ironically, I was born on Dr. Campbell's birthday and was delivered by him in the old Easy Street house. My weight was 5.2 pounds; without the help of Eagle Brand milk, I may not have made it. While there have been days when I wished the good doctor had had his way, obviously he missed his prediction on the physical health forecast.

Even more important than the abortion issue (though tied to it when prohibition folk argue that so many of the unwanted children become victims of neglect and direct abuse) is how we are treated after birth. And here is one of Saltville's greatest legacies. Our location in the mountain empire of Virginia with heavy Scotch, Irish and English descent, the Protestant work ethic, and rugged individualism made the caring and rearing of youth exceptional. Obviously, there were exceptions to this general practice, but by and large the stable, peaceful valley was a great place to be born and reared. As the Dutch say, "If you ain't Dutch, you ain't much." So Saltville folk had a pardonable pride and town-type confidence that made us "Saltville happy."

Athletics give community identity and rarely has a town centered itself more in athletics than Saltville. The nickname—Shakers—becomes unique and personal.

An incredibly level golf course in a high mountainous range, a cracker box type gymnasium (literally cramped by a stage on one end and stairwells boxing out the corner shots on the other end) and a spacious and beautiful baseball/football stadium all served to point out the fact that in Saltville, sports of all sorts was a way of life. Perhaps most symbolized and verbalized is Newt Williams' phrase carried on by Mack Blackwell and Don Morgan and similar to U.T.'s John Ward's call of, "It's football time in Tennessee." Thousands of Saltville fans have heard, "Here come those Shakers" as the 30 plus maroon-clad dudes entered the ballpark amidst Luroy Krumweide's 48-piece band blaring the popular fight song "Our Director" and to the words of "Three cheers for Saltville High School, maroon and gray..."

Thus, issues of "emotional murder" of youth were probably less in Saltville than any place in America. We were treated with good horse sense and our relatives also valued and loved "their horse"—especially if we could run a pigskin hard or hit a baseball long. As for "spiritual murder," which does occur through religious neglect, Saltville is perhaps well into being over-churched. Twelve churches exist in the corporate limits. While the plant, hospital and many businesses have closed since 1972, all the churches remain open. Neglect of the spiritual basics of worship, prayer, Bible study, and sharing time, talent and money are probably average in Saltville. The integration of faith and life seems to be exceptionally high. Pastor French Taylor showed much patience when he took the newspaper and Bible into a 1948 Bible school class and heard us racists belittle baseball's first black player Jackie Robinson for taking a "white man's job." Twelve years later, one of my first sermons was entitled "Bible and Segregation," a strong integrationist message, which met with little serious reaction in the church. Saltville's one percent black population, well employed and well behaved, reduced racism fears though the fears were never eliminated.

Small towns, unlike large cities, are low on crime in general and on murder in particular. The fewer the people, the bigger is the trust level among folk who are similar in nature and nurture. We simply did not choose to kill each other.

A myth of murder says people who are strangers and different kill one another more often. But the fatality stats figure most murders are in homes or places where the murderer and the victim are well known to each other, even related—as in the Bible's first murder of Cain killing his only brother Abel.

In Saltville, the family feuds stop well short of killing and we the people of Saltville in the words of the U.S. Constitution preamble "in order to form a more perfect union, establish justice, ensure domestic tranquility, provide for the common defense and promote the general welfare..." knew most about murder as we followed Raymond Burr and Perry Mason. And we, as Perry in the court cases, never lost many in killing in domestic or "stranger murders." Thank God we practiced one of the small town's top benefits—we did not kill.

Chapter 7

Birds and Bees meet Colored Balloons

Sex was and is as in most communities a highly popular but alternately public and private subject.

Some say our religion, sexuality, and finance are the top three private subjects of life.

"Private parts" was a popular Saltville cover term for those areas fig leaves tried to cover in the Garden of Eden. In our early years of curiosity, we tried to uncover, first as an Adam to an Adam and then as an Adam to some of the Saltville Eve's. Once playing the proverbial doctor's game, I recall as a child we had an "examining room" in a tent at the Sam Routh house on Easy Street. An unplanned massive spill of iodine in one of those areas now described by the anti-sexual abuse teacher as an area a two-piece bathing suit would cover sent us all scurrying in fear and frustration. It sent one of the patients to a real doctor and cost me as a disciplinary action by the home folks a scheduled trip that afternoon to Hungry Mother Park near Marion, a major trip in that day.

The good/bad news of Moses and the return from Sinai caps the sexual history of Saltville. Moses in returning from the mountain was reported by a Rabbi friend in some jest to have said, "I have good news and bad news concerning the commandments. The good news is I have him down to ten. The bad news is one of them is still adultery!"

There was a free flow of facts and fiction in Christian sexuality (probably an incompatible phrase in that period to even some religious folks). Mostly we learned of sexuality by jokes, exaggerations and a few textbooks peeked at from doctors' home libraries. Some will find it difficult to believe that our senior trip to Washington, D.C. in 1956 was the place where many of us saw our first copy of *Playboy Magazine.* In those days there was only a few carefully angled photos of pretty lassies.

The comic book cartoon booklets known only by a term too graphic for here were popular in our seventh grade class until Maude Moore intercepted one during a softball game and challenged the entire and embarrassed class to focus on "things pure and good."

Movies in those days required married couples to converse from double beds and the strongest word heard from either the old Victory Theater, operated by Tate Spraker, or its successor, the Salt Theater, operated by Wally Roberts, was Rhett Butler to Scarlett about not giving a damn about Scarlett's future.

Band director, Luroy C. Krumweide (son-in-law of the local Baptist pastor) shocked some band members in his frequent efforts at value setting and musical discipline. During a broom sale for band funds (yes, we did it then, too) he would say in reference to our indifference to sales, "You don't seem to give a tinker's dam." He quickly explained that a tinker was a person who repaired washing tubs with bolted-type washers which were called dams.

Many were the "dirty" or sex jokes around Saltville—
some imported and some obviously home grown. I
wondered then and now why we called them "dirty"
jokes since all could be considered dirty in their intent
and tone. But any joke concerning sexuality and reducing the creative and loving process to a dirty subject
should offend us and perhaps explains some of the un-
resolved sexuality of Saltvillians and the rest of the
world.

A strong joke then but a mild one today was overheard by us fellows when Pete Frye, the barber, asked
Roy Yontz in the older barber shop one afternoon if he
knew the riddle where does a bee put his stinger at
night? Pete's jovial answer was "In his honey." The OK
Barber Shop and later Hayden's Barber Shop were
havens for discussions of sexuality, politics, athletics,
finance, religion and related humorous yarns. So strong
were the subjects and opinions expressed that fist fights
and at least one "Coke bottle crowning" occurred.
Debate over union management issues became so intense that a realignment of barbers lead to a mostly
management shop (Joe Vernon's) and a mostly union
shop (Roy Hayden's). Today there is one shop with two
barbers named Joe Vernon, age 88 with 67 years of cutting hair, and the same Roy Hayden, age 67 with 45 years
cutting hair.

Perhaps most shocking to this 12 year old in the
1950s was the exit by one barber shop person for an
afternoon rendezvous with "a lady of the night." He
returned with a locker room brag-type report and quickly received a plea from another barber shop person to
"set him up" that night. (Not actually the quote but close
enough for this publication.) Both men were well married with children in our age range. The openness to
whoever was present that day still amazes me.

The humor associated with the several subjects of barber shop debate locks in some well-known if not entirely accurate events. Dr. Thomas K. McKee, the patriarch of local medicine, farming and Democratic politics, was the author and/or butt of many a Saltville story. Two are vivid and relate to sex and aging. An aging farmer came to see the doc one morning complaining of the loss of sexual capacity. He asked if there was a pill or shot the doctor could give him for correction. The veteran and versatile doctor grumbled in his non-baptist introductory phrase, "By God, John, I'd give three of my farms for such a shot." Later that morning, the doctor had a similar inquiry from a fellow who used to sell illegal fireworks. The old doctor roared as he leaned on his cane sharing his answer with the barber shop shift. "I said, 'By God, man, sex is like those Roman candles you used to sell for years. There are just so many shots and that's all!'!"

A personal story summarizes my Mother's frustration and shares another of the good doctor's wittiness on his feet. Around 1945 in the doctor's office waiting area in the old Saltville Hospital, which occupied the upper floor of the old Mathieson General Store, we were waiting our turn to see another doctor. My younger sister, Sena, and I were wandering in those ether-saturated and brown-linoleumed hallways. As a tall and stately Dr. McKee approached, my seven-year-old insecurities drove me to my mother's knee. Sena was up the hall, scooting those old but beautiful oak-slatted chairs into a make-believe train row. I was as thin as a rail in the chair backs and Sena was pleasingly plump. The dialogue between Mother and Tom McKee went something like this:

Dr. McKee: "Ruth, why don't you feed that child clinging to your lap? You old damn cheap tight

Republican. See that girl playing with those chairs? Talk to her mother and feed that boy what she's feeding that girl."

Ruth McCready: (Thinking she finally had one on the skilled doctor, replied) "Dr. McKee, I'll have you to know that that girl and this boy eat at the same table, live in the same house, and have the same mother and father. Sena and Stan are brother and sister separated by just two years."

Dr. McKee: (Not to be outdone, retorted in his customary introductory phrase.) "By God, Ruth, are you right damn sure they have the same father?"

Adultery was common in Saltville with well-known or alleged unions which produced some of Saltville's finest. To name or hint at probable ones would add pain to folk who had enough both as kids and as "producers."

The absence of abortion on demand in those days allowed children to be born within existing families and beyond. The "shotgun wedding" or "seven-month pregnancy" was probably the same as the southern average with some being better known than others depending on the obvious facts and the degree of focus the general gossips chose.

One lady was famous for recording marriage dates on her special "birthday calendar." When the first-born child arrived after that marriage, she would check that child's birthday against the parents' marriage date. If less than nine months had passed, she gave the baby a red star, perhaps like the red "A" in Hawthorne's novel, *The Scarlet Letter*. She discontinued her bridal birthday calendar after her only daughter's first born earned a red star, and the calendar keeper came to really meet the forgiver of all misplaced passion, sex, gossip or any excess.

Saltville had much sexual expression beyond adultery. Adultery is a limited word but the seventh commandment amplified by the additional Old Testament Law and New Testament teachings would include additional sexual subjects of fornications (sex by the unmarried), masturbation (self sex) homosexuality (same sex, sex) and nocturnal dreams or wet dreams (involuntary fantasy self sex). We had lots of the first two and very little reporting of the latter three. We heard through locals of sex sharing from the late night Post Office step conversations to the barber shops and post-lunch huddles at the old high school.

Fornication gets very common from my first experience with an innocent neighbor partner when neither knew much about the act other than the most elemental. Birth control was our earliest introduction when finding condoms on the old path to town from our Easy Street shortcut that intersected what is now the flower shop and would have cut across the back of the funeral home lot. I remember vividly finding colored condoms on that path and also in the old open sewer creeks even when World World II limited rubber availability. I remember seeing my first balloon in 1946 when Mickey Taylor brought back six colorful ones from Bristol. One of my sisters made the neighborhood news when she found a colored condom on the path to town and was prevented at the last second from trying to blow it up as a balloon by a wiser peer.

The percentage of virginity among girls and boys was much higher in that era. No doubt the majority of males and females were at least technical virgins but any male sexually active was envied as a hero. But the sexually active girls were called whatever the then in-term for unpaid prostitution might have been.

I had a disappointing experience with one of the town's better known practitioners and shared that guilt along with dozens of our friends as she made suicide attempts and bore some children with the fathers perhaps known only to God—sort of an unknown father syndrome. The redeeming history at last report was that she was married to a decent man who accepted the children and both were serious in their faith and were involved in the church. How all that could happen is a spiritual salute to the small town grace and the big time acceptance of sexual sin in Saltville.

Masturbation is one of those practices or series of practices that almost all males do but few report comfortably. Three males among the many hundreds I have counseled claim they never did masturbate. Two are among the most totally healthy folk I know and one is institutionalized. I learned of the practice as a fifth grader on a camping trip overlooking the Ice Plant. It was a group instruction by an older seventh grade boy and would qualify as a very passive form of homosexual behavior. At that age and in that group setting most all counselors would call it highly normal. The abnormal occurrence for me was immediate enormity of the involved anatomy, sending me to Dr. Campbell the next morning, highly embarrassed. Scared but finally relieved to hear his diagnosis, he simply said, "Looks like a spider bite." The return to normal was both welcomed and disappointing! The nickname 'Spider' was shortlived so the list of the eight participants will not follow since all turned out well sexually and otherwise. I am sure they would rather their names not appear at all in this book than to appear in this chapter.

The churches, schools and even homes were not very helpful with sex education in general. Hence, from authorities that reasonable masturbation was healthy would have helped a lot of budding Shakers. We got the opposite one night in a response by a Bristol State Liner's right fielder who was also an educator. We were ribbing his play and he shouted back to an unusually fine bunch of teenage boys isolated down the right field line, "Why don't you all go home and play with yourselves." I don't think he meant card playing.

As universal as masturbation was in Saltville, homosexuality was seemingly well below the generally projected figure of ten percent of the population. Translated, of the 2,300 population of Saltville, 230 would be "gays." I use the word only for variety and an abbreviation for the seven syllable "homosexuality." Most gays are not gay or happy. Our 1956 graduating class of 48 would have to have had five to keep the percentages alive. Perhaps many of that era had to "come out of the closet" or stop repressing their early urges later in life, but this non-sheltered native and uninhibited conversationalist observed very little personal knowledge of Saltville's homosexuals. There are some I know and a few were probably in community leadership roles. Certainly they suffered the redneck put-downs of rejection and ridicule. I spoke some of that put-down stuff until I met, counseled and befriended a few of that ten percent number and came to feel indirectly their pain and the pain of their parents and siblings.

I do not know the practice in the McCready-DeBusk family tree though several of us and hundreds of Saltvillians fit into the family patterns that contribute to being not so gay in our male and female sex lives. As in the McCready-DeBusk families, perhaps Saltville is below the national average in this difficult to admit practice. Or perhaps some of the alcohol-drug abuse in a "dry"

Saltville and Smyth County is an effort to relieve the pain of a "queer" (not meant in a put-down spirit) sex drive. One could easily argue in great detail that Saltville offered a male's paradise for healthy young boy pursuits. Less for the girls in that day, but again with Audrey Hardin and Rene Helton challenging sports officials, girls and boys got more than enough athletic encouragement.

There were many good male role models in my early years, including Roy and Chub Arnold, Bill Totten, Les Brannon, L.C. "Whitey" Arnold, James Albert "Brub" Cahill, Coaches Leonard Mauck, Harry Frye, Jim Neblett, John Northern, J.C. Smith, and fellows on the street like Roy Maiden, Kyle Taylor, and fellows in churches like Luke Campbell, Claude Smith, and Uncle Dave Collins.

No doubt boys interested in pursuits like art or music were held in more contempt than we see nowadays and some of that was engendered by some of the Jeter Barker philosophy of calling band members piccolo players. The conflict over the use of the practice playing football field after school got so intense between Luroy C. Krumweide and Jeter Barker that Ray Worthy himself had to call them together and tell them to get along or get out. Taking typing or home economics in that day was rare with the male and perhaps subtly threatened by the Shaker roughman Marlboro image. But just as we have learned that real Marlboro country is the graveyard, we learned that Bermuda shorts on males or piano-playing men are not necessarily gay stereotypes. Harry Truman, the piano-playing president, disproved the latter and Sidney Canter broke the unofficial ban on Bermudas by wearing a long-cut pair down town around 1954. Nowadays mailmen wear shorts as official postal dress. However, in the 1950s it would have brought the roof down if Frank Bennett, Guy Cahill or Troy Slate had worn Bermudas on the job. A vivid *Sports Illustrated* article from Old Sportsman's Park in St. Louis where temperatures got into the 100s in the broadcast booth showed Harry Caray stripped down to boxer shorts describing the game. "Holy Cow!"

Perhaps another true story and an unusual visit will be enough said on Saltville and sex for now. Dr. C.C. Hatfield, veteran general practitioner in the Rich Valley-Saltville area, passed along this report especially for this chapter.

Dear Stan

In 1936 when I first started My General Practice in Saltville, most of the work was confined to house calls and nearly all the babies were delivered in the home. In all I delivered more than 3,000 babies, 60% were delivered in the home.

One of my good friends in one of the mountainous areas just over the border in Tazewell County consistently had an addition to the family every two years. On the third or fourth occasion this happened, I remarked to the father that I would be seeing him again in two years. He replied, "Doc, if this happens again, I'm going to hang myself." Nevertheless, in about two years I was called again to deliver another baby. After delivery was accomplished and everything was in good order, and I was prepared to leave, I said to the father, "You remember what you promised yourself if this ever happened again? I see you are still walking around." He replied, "Doc, as soon as I found that old lady was in the family way, I went out to the barn and got me a rope and went on up into the mountains and climbed up into a tree and sat there studying about it, and it occurred to me that I might be hanging an innocent man."

Doc

The Hatfield Story and a McCready trip gets at part of the glory and gore of Saltville sex. My wife Judy and I accompanied 13 older adults to Mount Pleasant, Kentucky, near Lexington to spend the night in a former Shaker settlement.

The religious Shakers were named in a mocking fashion because they had ecclesiastical expressions in their worship. The religious Shakers, not to be confused at all with the athletic Shakers, had the most successful utopian commune settlements in American history. Their four-fold doctrine of: (1) withdrawal from the world, (2) regular public confession of sin, (3) communal celibacy (no sex for any reason), and (4) pooling of all possessions made them both inviting and almost extinct. The War between the States and worldly attractions along with no reproduction or successful evangelism has lead to their almost complete demise. Today, there are only five elderly female Shakers alive in America.

Our visit showed their remarkable creativity, simple values, hard work, excited worship and insistence upon the highest quality of production. They shipped brooms, seeds, and preserved items as far south as New Orleans.

The lack of control, knowledge, or certainty of faithfulness in the father mentioned in Dr. Hatfield's story and the renunciation of sex by the religious Shakers shows Saltville and the world the confusion over God's greatest reproductive and love expression, sexuality. From Adam and Eve to John Holmes (a porn star who died in 1988 from AIDS), to the girl friends of Jim Bakker and the apparent prostitutes (paid?) of several presidents, sex is the wonderful but woeful experience too few ever truly experience as the Creator of Sex and Life outlined in his life and sex manual, the Good Book, as known at the ole Salt Works.

It is a journey for all of us, and many can thank Saltville for setting some boundaries and standards if not supplying all the answers or the best role models. The final illustration, I heard at the Old Ice Plant and have used in numerous frank counseling sessions. Our sexuality is similar to the dog and the dog's wagging his tail. It's normal and natural for a dog to wag his tail, especially when he is happy. It is abnormal, sick and ultimately destructive if the tail wags the dog. The way I first heard it had a little more graphics supplied, but the way I'm learning it through Biblican Christianity is that we indeed are to use our sexuality as well as all of God's gifts and not be used by them.

Chapter 8

Zagnuts and Heavy Thumbs

Stealing in Saltville was as popular as in other places, but because of the small town's capacity to focus on wrong and the Scotch Irish hard work ethic, it was more likely to be exposed. Coupled with the conservative religious faith, Saltville had less trouble at interpreting the eighth commandment than any of the other nine—do not steal. Three vivid experiences jump to my mind and conscience. Two were as victims and one was as violator.

Some of the second grade students in Miss Grayson Webb's middle building ground-floor classroom (always heavily oiled by Fremont Harris and Curtis Hunt) brought snacks for the daily recess period. Mine was usually peanut butter and crackers to go with that half pint of fresh milk which cost us a walloping three cents. One day at snack time I discovered to my unbelievable dismay that I had been robbed of the Ritz cracker peanut-butter covered five pack. Second grade gossip, being what it was, soon traced the missing treat to be in a certain student's desk. His being a good friend caused me further confusion. I recall crying about it, more out of hurt than anger, since a good friend had stolen something so small, and he could have had some of them if he had simply let me know his needs. I also learned from that incident (to further my eventual psychological confusion) that "big boys don't cry."

Stealing as a lark seemed to be our motive for a 24-candy bar heist from the ball park concession stand one off season. Several of Easy Streets' upright teens discovered the concession door wide open. In our haste and hesitancy to "lift," we settled on a box of Zagnut Bars, only to discover later as we tried to celebrate our windfall they were insect infested and five of the six "robbers" admitted we didn't even like Zagnuts. To this day, I remember the theft when I see a Zagnut Bar.

"Commercial honesty" was learned from the study of weights and measures in Helen Callihan's government classes to Dr. "Cee" Sammy Jones' oft-repeated story of getting robbed at the General Store Market, the forerunner to the Super X Market. The place itself was classic from the aroma of fried bologna (the fried bologna properly curled and coated heavily with bright yellow mustard on a hamburger bun was a local favorite). In Saltville, bologna was often referred to as "a cab driver's steak."

Between the meat-bar restaurant at the market and the steady flow of female shoppers comes "Cee" Jones with a story of a black man's falling victim to a white man's authority. The butcher, another wise, good man, a good Easy Street neighbor and good family man, was often direct if not curt in his sales mannerisms. "Cee" swears that one day he ordered five pounds of hamburger, and upon hearing his request, the frugal butcher yanked a piece of the oil-based white wrapping paper from a three-foot roller, slung a gob of burger meat on it, and placed the package on the scales. "Cee" and "Doctor Jones," the veteran hospital orderly, said anybody could see the mound of meat was well shy of five pounds when the needle settled toward three instead of five. "Cee" says the good butcher placed his trusty thumb on the scales and called out, "Five pounds even." This butcher's transition phrase to his customers was, "And now then, what else, fellow?" Cee said he always knew he had been "beat" when the old butcher called out, "What else, fellow!"

My uncle Charlie DeBusk, once a meat cutter, said the butcher had a thumb worth its weight in gold—a hundred times over. To the accuracy of these reports, this reporter cannot personally attest, but mother often shared her having to contest the good butcher's effort to pawn off badly withered produce. One day as the butcher pushed the package across the old marble topped counter, Mother countered, "Sir, why don't you take this stuff and have your wife throw it out in her garbage...save me the trouble and cost of doing it myself." Upon which she swears her good neighbor said, "O.K. now, what else fellow?"

In balancing some defense of the General Store's honesty issue comes a wealth of customer beats the company reports. I'll always remember the rubber shortage of World War II and a compulsion I had to take an inner tube to the Hardy Roberts Memorial Swimming Pool for swim and play. I got hold of a rotten inner tube; and after buying a thirteen-patch kit and using all of them, I still was losing plenty of air. I went down to the old filling station where Ted Roberts had sold me the first kit and asked for another one. After hearing my story as to why I needed a second kit, instead of selling me one, Ted quietly walked over to the filling station warehouse (then on the lot of the later-to-be built Super X Market), pulled out a used but not rotten inner tube and simply gave it to me.

Squire Duncan, in his job of estimating the stockpiling of coal along the railroad tracks near the school house, had Rodney McCready as his assistant. They would measure the height and width of the various piles of coal and then estimate the inventory. One day Squire figured a hundred and ten tons of large chunk coal and then said, "Well, take off twenty and that makes ninety tons." Rodney asked, "Why do we take off twenty?" Squire smiled and said, "Well, we have to figure what some of our good citizens take each winter."

I can personally attest to heavy non-authorized discounts given to me and members of my family by a very congenial, accommodating clerk in the clothing department of the Mathieson General Store. I thought this clerk might be trying to help a poor large family, but then Ron Coulthard, whose father was well employed, reported the same 20 plus discount on every purchase. The other regular clothing clerk, a mild mannered, dedicated man whose affectionate by-word was, "Yes, uh huh," had annual sales well below those of the accommodating clerk. Store managers Hedley Craft and Glen Dalton may never have known why we preferred the accommodating clerk's service to the mild mannered, dedicated one. In this instance, who was guilty of stealing? Was it the customer who accepted the discount or the clerk who gave the unauthorized discount?

Stealing through tax cheating had few options in Saltville in the 1950s, for Virginia was one of the last states to adopt a retail sales tax which is hard to evade, and the income tax was not administered locally. Beating the revenuer's tax by moonshining in many Saltville mountains was very common during prohibition, and, to a lesser degree, it still exists today. But the "bootleggers" commanded most of the illegal liquor sales and evaded government prosecution, since bootlegging was a practice of buying Virginia State government liquor properly taxed and then re-selling it at a higher cost. Without any tax, sales occurred from homes, cabs, and one to one.

Since most likely our readers are not currently tithing ten percent of all income to the church, plenty of that form of stealing (withholding the tithe) was done in Shakertown. Saltville had fair financial church support with full time pastors at Madam Russell, United Methodist, First Christian, the Allison's Gap Church of God, the Saltville Presbyterian Church, the Saltville Baptist Church, and St. Paul's Episcopal Church as well as Main Street Christian Church. They were full time if you count circuit, combinations, retired and student supplied pulpits as full time. Saltville may have been the only town of its size in all of the Southland to have a Union Baptist-Presbyterian Church. Usually the Baptist Church is the strongest church in the community and would never be in a position to have to share a building. The frame building near the Well Fields was a Union Church shared by the respective Baptist and Presbyterian pastors on alternate Sundays. During the 1950s, we called it the "leaning church of Saltville" as it tilted front forward several degrees because of the Well Field ground shifts. It became the victim of fire in November 1967, never to be rebuilt.

Being a corporation town, more indirect stealing took place by the industrial age's new phenomenon called "beating in time." "The plant," as Olin and its predecessors were called, or as Dave Eastridge's kids would say, "Dad is at the 'works,'" had the largest volume of stealing. From "government jobs" like the hundreds of pipe cross-welded clothes line poles that dot the Saltville landscape to the surplus furniture like Dad's oak desk, which has followed me through eight parsonages, we all benefited and were guilty. (There is a set of clothes line poles still at the old McCready home of Easy Street or First Avenue.)

Corporation workers often rationalized (or as Notchie Cregger would say "figured") that we were underpaid and deserved some "self determined benefits." But the single largest stealing was loafing, sleeping or beating in time on the job. In the massive structure of the Olin Plant, there were many good hiding and sleeping places.

Buck Arnold relates how even the night watchman was tempted. His report may sum up a great deal of "indirect theft" and "borrowed religion."

A true story of Olin watchman, Ed Wix, began with his sleeping on the job one 11 to 7 shift with his head in hands. His supervisor, Frank Surber, came in to the watchman's shack quietly; but oddly, Ed brought his head up as Frank entered, and through bleary eyes said, "Praying for you, Frank, praying for you."

This 1946 aerial shot shows post war expansion. The upper left is being graded for the construction east of the barber shop (Aerial photo by Olin from Tom Totten collection).

The lower right has the "Alkalite" theatre at current town hall location, the old jail, the old, old post office and Pete Routh's dry cleaning shop at the former Piggly Wiggley location. The extensive parking area between the current library and the old jail was done for the 1932 Smyth County Centennial Celebration and is grassed over from rare usage. The depot and Power Company building flank the four Norfolk and Western rail track beds. Top center is the framed Mathieson General Store building (and sign) with the hospital occupying the upper floor.

Saltville, Spring 1964 with Olin Well field pump houses in the background. The "bucket line buckets" and tower in the foreground. Madam Russell Church and former parsonage to the right and a crowded business down town and rail section to the left (Photo by Tom Totten).

An incredible number of Saltville men at Sunday School
(Photo from Tom Totten collection).
Coach Leonard Mauch taught a Men's Bible Class in the late 1940s. They must have met in the sanctuary. The author did not realize that many men went to church anywhere in Saltville.

Dr. Thomas Kittsmiller McKee (Photo from Tom Totten collection).

Dr. Cecil Curtis Hatfield (Photo from Tom Totten collection).

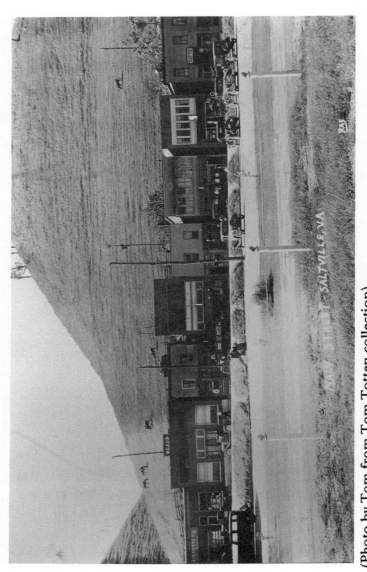

(Photo by Tom from Tom Totten collection)

This 1936 Main Street photo reveals the cattle on a cleared hill. Notice that Faucettes was once located in Saltville. On the far right was our Jewish merchant, Luckmann, whose business luck reversed when he helped A.B. Levine set up shop four stores to the left. Luckman was then sent packing to Richlands. Wheeler Farris began business on this side of the street in the "Big Restaurant". Note the dated cars and 1926 "Saltville Savings Bank".

A 1969 panoramic view of Saltville, Virginia (Photo by Tom Totten).

Ray Bonner Worthy (Photo from Tom Totten collection).

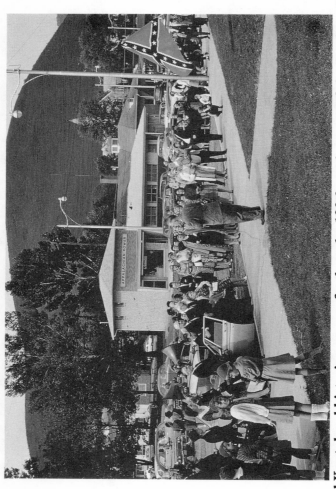

Bill Kent, local historian, pours forth at the 100th anniversary of the Battles of Saltville observance 1864-1964. How many home folk can you pick out allowing nearly 30 years? (Photo by Tom Totten)

Madam Russell United Methodist Church, the namesake of Elizabeth Henry Campbell Russell, the mother of Methodism in the Salt Lick Valley. She was the sister of Patriot Patrick Henry and wife to the Revolutionary War Generals William Campbell and William Russell. (Photo by Tom Totten).

Philosopher H. Kyle Taylor and Wife Mary (Taylor Family Photo).

The world's longest tramway (9.2 miles). The locals dubbed it the "bucket line," here framing most of the town with majestic Red Rock Mountain in the background (Photo from Tom Totten collection).

Stan McCready hauls Betty Soyars dressed in mother "Bill's" finest on somebody's sagging wagon [(1948) Soyars family Photo].

The former McCready Easy Street residence (current) showing the Bill Kent house only 20 feet apart (Photo by Stan McCready).

Victory Theatre projector operator, Doug Cregger,
snapped this shot of the author, his son Mike and the
deceased son of the "Dan" Tuckers, Little Tommy, from
Lover's Leap, 1945. Note unoccupied intersection which
now bears Saltville's only traffic light (Photo by Doug
Cregger). 1945).

A similar view shows changes in the past 50 years from the same angle on Lover's Leap, July 13, 1992 (Photo by Michael Stone).

A lowly son (Stan) laments his father's death surrounded by his father's flowering porch plants — especially morning glories (McCready Family Snap Shot).

Sister Sena and Stan illustrating the weight contrasts used in the Dr. McKee and mother Ruth confrontation (McCready Family Snapshot).

The McCreadys at Stan and Judy's wedding, March 9, 1974, Galax, Virginia. (left to right) Haynes Meadows 1929 - 1991 Blake Tarlton 1925 - 1975 Sena Kay 1940 Ruth DeBusk 1903 Mabel June (Whiz) 1933 Donald DeBusk 1923 - 1979 Rodney Cameron 1931 Stanley Carlton 1938 -

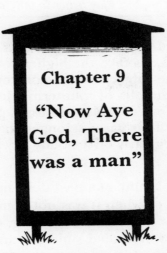

Chapter 9

"Now Aye God, There was a man"

The term false witness suggests a negative presence of evil or an absence of the truth. Lying is negative and the absence of truth. Silence in the face of evil is the absence of witness. Let's play these vague phrases out in the concrete, asphalt and blue grass of Smyth County's second largest town.

Saltville and the Bible are well supplied with multiple individual and group examples of false witnessing. An early Holy Writ writing is Cain's murder of his brother, Abel, and his poor efforts to excuse himself by trying to avoid God's question with a question, "Am I my brother's keeper?"

A good Baptist and church history professor, Clarence Goen, posed a question from Wesley Seminary, Washington, D.C., that rang loud in the 1960s from the nation's capitol all the way to the "Holy City" of Saltville, "Am I my brother or sister's brother?" Listing Saltville's false witnesses would include almost all of us at some stage in life.

Those areas important for a true witness are common to Shaker Town, but we had some very uncommon witnesses. Categories which lead to a false witness will bring to mind ideas, events, and folks who would be clear examples. Let's take the higher road, however, in print, and list the subjects which confront the false witness and offer examples of countering the evil result and returning good for evil. False witness is primarily fueled by the following four gases stronger than any chlorine we woke up to regularly on a cloudy day in the Corporation Town:

(1) Malice: I think of a next door neighbor who suffered divorce when it was not common. Being left with four children, including two toddler twins, one of whom died suddenly and tragically, she came back home to live with her aging parents. Her mother, once a vibrant and loving lady (who, in my pre-school days, daily made me great biscuits from scratch and spread them hot with cow butter) had become a physically and mentally incapacitated bed patient. Our identical houses were separated by only 22 feet. She was a faithful mother, daughter, choir member, and simply a beautiful type neighbor—a true witness. She was the only daughter of Bill and Era Kent— Frances Marshall Kent Crawley Short. Frances Marshall's works updated Abraham Lincoln's words with one to one relevance, "With malice toward none..."

(2) Fear: Franklin Delano Roosevelt's words from a depressed nation's Capitol Building on a snow-swept set of steps had less application for Saltville than any place I have never known—"We have nothing to fear but fear itself." Fear as a heavy false witness in Saltville seems to have been overridden by economic security (when the corporation was strong), a Scotch-Irish rugged individualism

mentality, a confident set of religious options, and perhaps other conditions unknown to me. Rarely did I hear it as a motivation for getting right with God, studying books, practicing health care, or appearing in personal issues. True, we had our folk afraid of storms, diseases, blacks, and other fear-producing subjects, but most Saltville house doors were not locked regularly! Our old home place had to have locks added when I sold it. In 30 years, I never had a house key for the home place located two blocks from down town Saltville.

An educational transplant to Saltville helped many youth to drop the walls of fear with the use of sports and, in the general culture. After a 1947, 9—0 football season ended with a 50—0 shocking loss to the then prime rival, county seat Marion, he lost his head-coaching job to the "boo birds."

He showed us many practical ways and reasons to overcome fear in scouts, camping, swimming, body shyness, travel, and in other natural settings from classroom to gridiron that helped plant seeds still bearing fruit against unreasoned fear. I served as his pastor in nearby Glade Spring where he took sanctuary from the Saltville firing. The Shakers' loss was a great gain for our western neighbors. His intensive time with younger boys was part of his needs and our needs, as well as was his ministry. I had occasion to check out his character indirectly dozens of times through fellows from both areas, and only found the gossips had greatly exaggerated his alleged false witness. Affectionately known as Coach he may have been the all-around sharpest and most sensitive fellow in those parts in those years. Elmo Early died in 1983 at age 67.

(3) Careless: The difference between being a false witness and a good one may hinge around being careful rather than careless. "I don't know and I don't care." These twin barrels of anti-care and anti-knowledge are fired regularly in the Holy City as in any locale from Eden to Tiananmen Square, China."

Saltville took public education and religion seriously. The town had a separate school system which Olin supported by supplementing the teachers' salaries. The extended search for a strong and long-staying principal, expressed through Lynn F. Moore, personalized the school board's determination. Mrs. Lenora Richardson's long and faithful tenure and her salary support from Saltville churches and citizens proved invaluable to the town because she taught the Bible to those who never went to Sunday School. That great program started after my elementary days, but two things ring loud the bell of care through Mrs. Richardson's ministry. Her showing and narrating her dream trip to the Holy Land was made Saltville relevant when she came, a bit embarrassed, to this minister. She quietly but firmly reported a golf course statutory gang rape of one of her current female students by seven of our athletes. The victim had come to Lenora in great hurt. I talked Dutch uncle style to my generation gap buddies, and we decided, after some real shame on all participants' parts, that legal action was not a proper course.

Jesus' words to the woman (girls and the boys) "Go and sin no more" were never quoted by the Bible teacher, but that was the concluding spirit which permeated beautifully on this ugly event.

In a much lighter vein, Bob Chapman tells of the oft heard story illustrating carelessness, ignorance and persistence.

Joe Pickle was one of the many Saltville suburbanites (Allisons Gap) who came to the town each spring with a plow, harrow and a team of mules. During those days, people had larger gardens and neither power mowers or rotary tillers. The spring plowing was popular and profitable for the equipped farmers.

Joe was contracted to plow and harrow the garden of a strict work ethic widow who had electrified her adjoining fence unknown to Joe. Each time he took a break from a few furrows to mop his brow, he leaned against the 500 volt fence and got a healthy shock. Slowed down and frightened, Joe was confronted for his slow progress. The wage-conscious widow was paying by the hour or minute as many depression graduates paid in those days. She rushed Joe, just after this third electrical encounter, and asked why he was jerking so hard and plowing so slowly. As he headed his mules toward the wagon, quitting the job in mid-furrow, he replied in a loud frustrated voice, "My God, woman, I've done had three heart attacks, and I quit."

(4) Silence: A most exacting false witness story comes from the hey-days of Saltville's "Sodom" section—so called by the fire eating preachers in the 1930s and '40s because of the loose ladies and the

free flowing booze—Henry Town's taverns or the Warfield Saloon. A local citizen of questionable character had agreed to witness for the prosecution on an illegal liquor sale. The man accused was named Lonnie Shupe. Somebody got to the witness before court time, and when the judge asked why he had said Lonnie Shupe was guilty earlier, and now he was not sure about it, the witness replied without blinking, "Oh, Mr. Honor, all I said to the po-lice-mun was, 'Mr. Jingo Lambert, I saw a little short man,' not Lonnie Shupe."

(5) Half truths: Our major court promise, "to tell the truth, the whole truth and nothing but the truth," with the traditional hand on the Bible, may have roots in this ninth commandment. This is a legal and spiritual challenge if not an impossibility.

Only "mayor's court" with minor cases was held in Saltville; thus there are few court cases for reporting. But practical truth about persons good and bad would clearly be the challenge of the amplification of this commandment in the 1940s to '60s.

One Saltville transplant who exemplified this issue was the late Newt Williams. His nature created many friends and foes. As a kid I heard the foe stuff, particularly centering around his assigned membership in the head football coaches' "big four cabinet." This group was alleged to have enormous influence in the athletic program of the then Saltville High School. Other members were believed to be Turk and Gray Warren, and Joe Fields.

We saw Newt's worst side or perhaps some half truth when a bunch of us baseballers were swigging Pepsis from the 12-ounce long neck bottles partly filled with peanuts. As we sat lounging on Myrtle Tilman's green outside that huge hedge, Newt passed by slowly in his old black Chevy. He nodded pleasantly, but Bob "Little Boozie" Booth responded loud enough for us to hear and hopefully not loud enough for Newt to hear, "Hi, Coach!" Newt stopped, backed up the old Chevy, and with a clear change of countenance firmly challenged Bob, "What the hell gives you the license to call me names?" Bob swallowed his peanuts and softened his comment to little avail from Newt's view.

These "coaches" were great supporters of a great athletic program. Their tireless and volunteer efforts gave kids like us something good to do. Perhaps they were over zealous and even interfering, but they cared and acted on it. Don Parks quit football one afternoon, and Turk was in his home that night encouraging his return.

Newt was a special example of how one could use personality traits and other people could construct an unlikable person before you ever came to know him on your own. I overheard him invite one of the poor Hart Spring Hollow boys to move his bank account after the fellow mildly complained to a female teller about a banking error. I thought it harsh on an underprivileged young adult then. But in more mature years, I learned we need to tell folks how we feel and occasionally suggest they pay a visit to the darker regions. 'Tis healthier than suppression leading to depression.

But the fuller truth on Newt was his unparalleled success as Saltville's representative to the Smyth County legislative body—the County Board of Supervisors.

His original election victory was over brother Rodney, who most would say was more popular than Newt. Also, Rodney's being a Republican in Saltville at the time would have made him the clear favorite. Newt not only won handily but was re-elected more times (20 years) to that board than any person in history.

Rodney's favorite story about losing to Newt goes: "I got 359 votes, Newt got 575 votes, and at least 600 people have told me they voted for me." Rodney never doubted the truth of the election officials' count. He worked with them for 12 years and six elections. He did wonder about the full truth of the voters' conversations.

Newt coined and popularized the grammatically correct, "Here come those Shakers," his introduction to the football team preceding the game time entry.

A listing of the top ten true witnesses of Saltville's Biblical Truths for me follow in alphabetical order. Picking an arbitrary limit of ten for the Saltville True Witness Hall of Fame is like fishing in Tumbling Creek on a good day when you get your limit early. Oddly, five of the chosen are dead and five are living. These then were chosen from my years of Saltville recollection from 1945 to 1965. There are so many more who deserve listing here, but a larger number than ten is more than this writing can handle.

E. Roy Arnold, Sr. (1903 - 1981)

Roy represents the clergy as a member of the Christian Church in part-time ministry. His six-boy family, coupled with a local Booth girl known as Virgie, stands out for varied reasons. He was uneducated but wise. (Faithful in churches though many of his folk were uncustomarily contrary.) Roy played a larger role in fathering care than most despite his two full-time jobs: his pastoring and his plant work. His dropping by on Sunday mornings to take brother Rodney to church was normal evangelism. But Roy and Claude M. Smith's visit to me when I was suffering vocational indecision and personal depression was second-mile pastoral care since Roy was not my pastor. I first remember him in our home in 1946 when he came to repair a radio in time for the Red Sox-Cardinal World Series. His varied skills and compassionate heart outweighed his pronouncing the "T" in apostles and his critics' charge that he was not "mean enough" from the pulpit. I was privileged to help bury Roy. The always reverend and relevant E. Roy Arnold perhaps buried more Saltville natives than any other area minister in memory. So from a friend still this side of the Elizabeth Cemetery, "Rest well, 'lad' (his term for males) you earned it from the plant to the pulpit."

Mabel Crabtree Clear (Mrs. Guy) (1911 - 1990)

Our Easy Street neighbor was a math teacher and Madam Russell organist for forty years. She last appeared publicly at the organ bench where her fatal stroke hit her as she was preparing for still another worship service.

From the strict teaching of math to the daily classroom reading of the devotional guide *The Upper Room*, she was organized and dedicated. Her once a year variation from homework, boardwork, and paper grading saw her bring her accordion for the pre-Christmas in-class music concert.

We often mused about and then later appreciated her enthusiastic leading of the classroom cheer, as she cocked her thumb and index finger each Friday before the big game and led us, "What's the matter with our team? It's all right." Mabel, or "bone face," as her cruel critics privately called her, was more than all right. She would laugh at the preacher's jokes when nobody else laughed. I once branded her my worst teacher. (She failed me with a 68 in algebra I, but I had cheated for most of that.) Brother Haynes said that probably meant she was one of the best teachers in the system, and indeed she was. So Saltville bade farewell to one of its dearest sisters in 1990 when Mabel, without accompanying text, organ or accordion, joined Guy (they were biologically childless) probably singing, "On Jordan's Stormy Banks I Stand and Cast a Wistful Eye, Oh Who Will Come and Go With Me..." They were, indeed, one of the greatest teams of church leaders, on-the-job workers, neighbors and citizens ever to grace old Easy Street or all of the Saltville Valley. Mabel and Guy, there is nothing wrong with your team.

Dr. C.C. Hatfield (1908 -)

Cecil Curtis Hatfield, country boy who did well as a town doctor, financier, community leader and dry humorist, is another sometimes misunderstood true witness. His father James Hatfield was from the North Holston area, his mother Sarah Osborne Hatfield was from Little Valley, and they raised their son Cecil Curtis in McCready's Gap.

Uncle Charlie DeBusk would laughingly tell how sheltered and even confined Curtis as a kid was "put into a bonnet and fenced in like a dog. Why, he would run back and forth along the fence 'til he wore a path." This story temporarily prejudiced me, but Mother would always challenge Uncle Charlie's account by explaining that the Hatfield's had lost several children in early deaths and were being justifiably careful with their only surviving child.

Well, "Doc," you cut a mighty good path from Rich Valley to Saltville and beyond.

He had delivered 3,332 babies, most in homes from 1935 to 1969. Today he has a stack of index cards 22 inches high which represent unpaid patient bills. He says the greatest advance in general medicine was the advent of sulfa drugs and penicillin, and he claims the strangest refusal of medical advice he ever received came from a Saltville man whose testicles needed to be removed. "No, Doc, I can't let you do that. I think they look good on a man."

Since 1949, he has been actively involved in the business activities of the First National Bank of Saltville, serving as president from January 8, 1963, to January 9, 1990, and currently serving as a member of the Board of Directors.

"Doc" and Peg's only son Jim has chosen to follow the banking business as his career.

"Doc's" broad participation in the community has included involvement in a rural church, the community college, mental health issues, the Welfare Board, Scouting, Kiwanis, and especially the Saltville Rescue Squad of which he was charter member and served as president for several years. In 1991 he became an honorary member of the Rescue Squad and presently functions as a medical adviser.

He has made the lives of countless Valley folk better from delivery to loans to laughs. (His best story appears in the Adultery Chapter.)

So, "Doc," thanks for helping us then and, in Saltville "ese," thanks for helping us "still yet!"

Ruth DeBusk McCready (1903 -)

Farm girl Ruth, who at 17 married Wyndham, a local product of the industrial age, was widowed during World War II with seven living children from pre-school Sena to college age Don along with brother, Blake, in the Pacific Theater of War. She set a classic example of determination and stoic compassion. This high school educated, hard-working lady is still perking at 89. She has helped bury her husband, parents, five children and seven of her ten siblings.

Mrs. John H. (Maggie) Moore (deceased: dates unavailable)

Another transplant proves Saltville does not have a monopoly on ministers of true witness. The acting elementary principle and veteran southern lady circulated well without a car in the family. Harvard graduate and husband John H. rode his famed bicycle to the plant daily and Maude hoofed one mile to school, rain or shine. They were non-conformists in many meaningful ways. For example, they were Southern Baptists to the core when the Baptist Church was ranked sixth in local church strength with no more than 20 regular worshippers in 1955. Her style and thoroughness in teaching was never paralleled in my educational odyssey of the Saltville system, Emory and Henry College, Candler and Wesley Theological Seminaries, though each of those schools were strong and well staffed. She covered every subject thoroughly and regularly and I could never tell which subject or students she liked best.

She believed in classroom entertainment and allowed us to hear the closing innings of a World Series game and Douglas McArthur's "Old Soldiers Never Die Speech" to Congress on that stately old radio in the shapely cabinet frame with the church window architecture. The RCA was located just to the left of her desk (pulpit) which looked like an electronic lectern. She was a forerunner of high-tech teaching. She read aloud classics like *Uncle Tom's Cabin* and *The Christmas Carol* chapter by chapter, and we listened with fervor. She had us all stand four-square before the class and repeat verbatim Lincoln's Gettysburg Address and The Presidential Oath of Office. To my knowledge, no class member has ever needed to take that oath of office.

We even had a mock trial to experience a civics class lesson of judge, jury and witness. She even yielded to our ridiculous pressure of trying Harry Truman for firing Douglas McArthur. Because of the intense interest much of the class held, she went along with the idea. Her religious fervor required all witnesses to alter the truth oath as we repeated, "I swear to tell the truth and nothing but the truth so help me George Washington."

President Truman escaped conviction by us radical Republicans when Violet Allison hung the jury one to eleven. Staunch democrats Kyle Taylor and Maude Moore were pleased with our fervor and with the outcome. Mrs. Moore relinquished her "pulpit" only to Luroy C. Krumweide once a week for music and to Principle Ray Buchanan and Dr. Soyars once for an embarrassed male only one hour sex education presentation. That hour was the least new material ever presented in her cathedral of learning.

I never learned more depth and more variety in one school year anywhere, and it was largely due to one experienced, well-rounded and determined teacher. She taught some other lessons like the day Bill Booth kept staying in the boys' rest room, and she, being inconsistent with her soft style, had to raise her voice saying, "Who's in there?" Bill responded, "There ain't nobody in here." She said, "Bill, do not say 'ain't and you are somebody. Always remember that."

An uncle, Dr. Fred DeBusk, enroute to one of his 30 consecutive World Series vacations, called Mrs. Moore one night from our home. I overheard him saying, strange to me at the time, "Mrs. Moore, I just wanted to thank you for helping me along so well, as my seventh grade teacher." Those were words from a million dollar California surgeon to a two thousand a year Saltville teacher. And, Mrs. Moore, may I call you Maggie, like Bear Bryant used to say on the telephone commercial about his mother, I sure wish I could call you and thank you for the help you were to me and many a Sal'vil...Sorry, Mrs. Moore...*Salt*ville...student. Teach them well up there.

Clarence Franklin "Con" Smith (1934 -   )

The Bass Smith roll call poem takes real flesh in this grandson. "Con," son of Alf and Anna Smith, is a proud servant who crossed the Henrytown (suburb) Bridge into a richer fuller day through self-determination, self-education, and ultimately self-dedication to the Father-God.

Two wall hangings symbolize his geographic and spiritual heritage. From his realty office, once a dental officer where Mary Virginia Coe made fillings and Dr. Baltimore drilled Saltville pearlies punctuated by his famous closure line, "Now spit that out."

Back to Con's office and the plaque which reads: "It's hard to be humble when you're from Henrytown," to penetrating photo of the mountain boy from North Carolina, the Reverend Billy Graham.

Con married Pattie Sturgill. Their children Norah, Pete, Joy, and Frankie still grace his life and stories. Frankie was killed in a cycle accident in 1986, and over 1,500 people came to help them grieve the death. Con's faith was an inspiration to the grievers.

His greatest lessons in life came early as he became the reading eyes for his merchant/taxi driver dad. "Meet your word" and "pay your debts" came from father Alf. A determined boy decided at the age of 11, "I can make it in business. I will not work for someone else when I can work for myself."

In 1951, he began washing cars for "Red" Sauls at 50 cents an hour. Since then, he has owned two service stations, various related auto supply businesses, unnamed commerical and residential property, and land holdings predicated on his axiom, "I give service." "My goal has never been dollars, but serving people faithfully has led to the security I sought. Even when I knew Olin would close down and my biggest account (Olin) and many individuals would have to move away, I started buying property because I believed in Saltville, myself and the good Lord."

After declaring (as Job) "If I lose my home, my holdings, my health or my family, I will not turn my back on Christ. I'm strongest there."

Well, Con, son of Alf, you did and are doing mighty well to get rich materially and spiritually and to keep the faith in Saltville and the good Lord. Thanks for coming across the Henrytown Bridge and helping others bridge their rivers and gaps.

It is hard to be humble when you're from Henrytown and Saltville.

Kyle Taylor (1908 - 1975)

Harold Kyle Taylor, the perennial cab driver philosopher and reformed alcoholic, had no regular nickname other than "Big Kyle" though he was not a real tall person or a fat man. I began his 1975 funeral with the sentence perhaps tabbing his real reason for being called 'big,' "Saltville's Will Rogers is dead at 67." Kyle, like

Will, was not a member of any organized political party.
He was always a Democrat!

Kyle called me aside immediately after my announcement of entering the ordained ministry and said,
"Aye God, McCready, (he never did use my first name)
will you bury me? I hate like hell to ask a damn
Republican, but there ain't nobody else that would or
that I'd have." The ego honor of a 23-year-old kid was
tempted but my evangelistic concern and "learned
graphic language" from Kyle caused me to reply, "Kyle,
old buddy, I'd be honored to put you under, if you will
let me work on you between now and then so we can get
you the right forwarding address on your coffin."

Kyle, through the prayers and labors of others, did
profess the faith in his latter years. I remember vividly a
visit before a Shaker homecoming game at his Main
Street home. He was on oxygen for emphysema and
answered me in his usual convincing style but in a nearly
silent voice. "I met Him and all is well with my soul."
These words were assuring but the death rattling cough
which followed reminded us both of his too many
"Lucky Strikes," which may have meant fine tobacco but
terrible health. Kyle may have been blinded to the organized church's valid role in Saltville by some of the
false witness actions of us hypocrites. Cab drivers expe-
cially have an angle on the seamy side of any community
including its church and non-church folk.

But he was not as blind as many of us to the physical
needs of people, thus a true Christian and true Democrat. His weighed reasoning and wealthy insight inter-
spersed with applied humor made him our true Will
Rogers. Since Kyle's wisdom appears amply illustrated
throughout this book and since I nearly named it
Saltville, Big Kyle and the Ten Commandments, a "Big Kyle"

put down story would be appreciated by him, now in the Big Sky Country.

During the pegged pants era, a big footed Shaker came strolling by the cab stand. Kyle asked, "Son, how in the hell do you get into those tight jeans over those big feet?" The slow-speaking teenager replied respectfully, "The same way you get your T-shirt over your big nose, Mr. Taylor." All of the sudden, Kyle had a quick cab call to make. That was the only time I heard Kyle outpointed verbally.

As I said at his funeral, Kyle Taylor offered much to his family, town and country. They did not always have the wisdom or timing to receive it. He offered the church (he really had no church) very little. What kind of youth counselor or men's Bible teacher he could have been will never be known, or as L.A. Dodger announcer, Vin Scully (Kyle hated the Dodgers) would say after the TV camera focused on a player who had missed an opportunity to drive in a run, "Of all the sad words of tongue and pen, the saddest are what might have been." But Kyle gets my "Saltville Hall of Fame" vote for his many important hits as we remember Kyle's record and our own. Nobody bats 1,000. "Why, hell, McCready, 280 will get you into baseball's Hall of Fame nowadays."

Kyle, old buddy, you were right about building fires in the White House and in declining a write-in election victory for conscience's sake. Let me confess to you that your influence and concern for the poor and your pride of the Southland has caused me to vote proudly for three Democrats for president (of southern origin, of course). Perhaps you and your descendants, like Pete Frye's daughter would have that doubt in common when I shared that fact at the door of First Christian Church in 1984. She looked a bit unbelieving and quickly wittedly said, "Pete would love to hear that but he would not believe it."

Kyle is probably shuttling Moses and St. Paul between appointments and saying, "Aye God, I finally made it." Well, "Big Kyle," thanks for the memories. You didn't outlive Bob Hope, but you left us enough Christian hope and horse sense to be proclaimed from your cab stand to hundreds of Holston Conference United Methodist pulpits. We look forward to seeing you and Mary when we ford Jordan's stormy banks. I would not be surprised if you don't meet us in one of your "rattleac cabs" with FDR sitting in the back seat puffing on a cigarette in his famous cigarette holder, with Pete Frye beside him giving him a presidential trim, and all of you joining in singing off key, but enthusiastically, "Happy Days Are Here Again." (Presuming that Pete, FDR and I cleared our accounts before the big pay day.)

W.J. Bill Totten (1908 -   )

Billy, as Bill Kent called him, was a native from the gap (Allison) and never a corporation employee. Bill did well in business, church, family, government and operated always with good Saltville horse sense.

Once known as "Fatty" Totten, Bill trimmed down and lost the insulting nickname. "Fatty," then, however, was a name of some affection as applied to "Fatty" Carter (Carl's father) and "Fatty" Cassidy.

Bill had early goals of saving money, $1,000 by age 18 and $30,000 by age 50. He achieved them but borrowed $65,000 a few years later. A thousand dollars in 1929 was a pot of money.

An early and wise businessman, he cherished friends of all ages, and never seemed dominated by the dollars he possessed. He sold me his Icon 1951 Pontiac in 1963 so I could have a car to serve four rural churches dotted around Emory and Henry College called the Emory Circuit.

The deal was legally signed for one dollar! Earlier, he paid all expenses for Pastor C.E Wilson to come and get me while I was suffering from acute personal depression at a youth camp in St. Simon Island, Georgia; and he sent a monthly check during my early seminary days.

His partnership with Charles Wiley was always strange to me since they seemed so different in politics, religion and personality. Even the drug store/furniture combination partnership seemed odd.

Bill married well with Litz of the Brickey girls and produced one of Saltville's finest and sweetest even spirited ladies of the 1950s when we called her "June Bug."

Bill's brief but productive tenure as mayor was marked by many achievements, but two odd ones hold my memory. Saltville's roads were atrocities. We kids were sure Mayor J.Q. Peeples got a kickback from local shock absorber sales. We had heard all the excuses of cost and shifting soil prohibiting good roads, but within a year of Bill's inauguration, every foot of primary road within the corporation of Saltville was smoothly paved.

Kyle Taylor who made his living by driving cab was glad for the improvement but said, "Them damn workers on the town water crew will have all these roads dug up in six months."

Cemeteries did not much interest us fellows in our teens except perhaps to play ghost games in them, but now I see why Bill listed clearing and cleaning of the town's Elizabeth Cemetery as one of his best deeds.

So, from his pew in Madam Russell to his counter at Totten's Drug Store, where I once haggled him down 50 percent for a girl friend's jewelry gift, to his desk at the town hall where he held my speeding case in his office to save me embarrassment and let me off with court costs and caution, to his countless similar acts of help and mercy to many of Saltville's various citizens, I say, "Yeah, Bill, you done mighty good" (to borrow a southern country expression).

Dr. Jerry Ray Willis (1940 -   )

I first saw Jerry Willis the day he was assigned to my Green Devil Pony League Baseball Team. The wiry, bespectacled kid with a blond flat top did not look athletically promising so I put him in right field to play the famed and difficult outfield which was largely a concrete tennis court. Years later he was named to two high school all-state teams in football and basketball—still a local record. The grandson of primitive Baptist elder, A.R. Singleton, and son of Thelma and Ray Willis, this Saltville transplant, originally from Kingsport, Tennessee, is one of Saltville's truest sons. He had one of the cleanest mouths and clearest minds, and taught me by debate, demeanor and practice, much in my six favorite areas of family, faith, education, athletics, sex, and politics. His brothers Joe and Johnny and son Lee have pioneered in the acceptance and able application of chiropractic health care in Southwest Virginia and South Carolina. His early swear phrase was, "sugar" instead of another similar sound, and he has sweetened lives of many with his determined progress and true witness in spite of early odds to the contrary. Jerry practiced and cheered the line commonly heard from the sidelines at Shaker athletic events, "Let's go, Shakes."

Ray Bonner Worthy (1891 - 1959)

Plant manager R.B. Worthy of McPherson County, South Dakota, became a household name in Saltville. Both labor and management people honored the stately Worthy by naming their children and their high school after him. One namesake, Bonner DeBord, the colorful, gangly and friendly son of James DeBord, carried out his name sake's golf interest by belting drives up to 350 yards. Worthy's interest in education, recreation, athletics and medicine, as well as families, is documented in these facts from the fifties:

(1) He was a school board member with true direction including the insistence of a top-rate high school facility with the construction of what was to be named Saltville High School but turned out to be his namesake.

(2) Detailed interest in a premier golf course, incredibly level in a range of hills and mountains, was only one of his recreational interests. I remember his asking me one day in a displeasing tone who it was he had spotted at a distance sunning on No. 9 green. I learned later it was Johnny Cregger, but "Little Notchie" had hightailed it to nearby Scotty Sauls' bushes when he saw the big man approaching by car.

(3) He helped obtain a high quality lighted athletic field, the first in our area, but told Alkali manager, Jim "Fodder Shock" Arnold, he would turn the park into a pasture field if the semi-pro (totally corporation-funded) team did not start winning. The Alkalis went on a 14-game winning streak. His concern for family was broadly illustrated in issuing jobs, retirements, and the ultimate break for the McCready family. His coffin-side assurance to a 43-year-old widow Ruth was, "Stay in this company house, rent free and maintenance free 'til your last child is educated." Sena, the youngest, was only five years old.

He lost his wife early, but reared three exceptional children, Pete, Dave, and Ellen. The presence of a local hospital with a surgeon and four general practitioners, coupled with a group insurance policy was part of his power and principle witness and care. Many of us never knew we paid doctors or hospitals until we left Saltville. Worthy was not an overt churchman by observable Saltville standards. He even drank and served the stuff in his house, the religious conservatives reported. But many of them came to appreciate his true witnessing as they learned that it covered more than church attendance and dietary practices. Mr. Worthy, as we were wont to address him, an industrialist/Republican, won the ultimate compliment from an Olin foe and populist Democrat Kyle Taylor, when Kyle said at Ray's death, "Now, Aye God, there was a man."

Chapter 10

Shakers Play Better in the Rain

We approach the last of the big ten commandments a little like a prize fighter in a ten-round match.

Saltville and the ten C's have sparred, pointed each other but neither has K.O.'d.

The athletic analogy fits Shakertown especially because the truest and fullest symbol of Saltville life is not overt religion but overt games—athletics.

Folk around Marion, Abingdon, Glade Spring and Bristol, Virginia used to say in a coveting way, "The babies at Saltville are born with a football in one hand and a baseball in the other." We were never accused of being basketballers in those days. I first learned to subtract on the old manual scoreboard at Shaker round ball games by placing the Saltville score under the opponent's score and mentally determining the point difference. We almost always had the smaller number. Our last round of oral history turned print material evolves around the common experience of athletics and centers on the rarely used term covet.

Covet means to want badly the possessions, abilities or traits of another person. I only remember hearing it once in those days and then in an acceptable positive way. Albert "Brub" Cahill was often told by people standing in the need of prayer, "Brub, I covet your prayers."

Covet from Mt. Sinai means eager desire for whatever or whomever is not properly our own. Coveting has three double first cousins and plays heavily in Peoria and between Plasterco and Poor Valley, as well as McCready's Gap in what some said should have been called Frye Town—incorporated Saltville. The popular cousins are greed, envy and jealousy. Most folk, including the Saltville citizens, would rank coveting as tenth on the list of Saltville sins until we consider her double first cousins. If envy is of things and jealousy is of people then greed is for possessing things and people. Remember there was a war fought in Poor Valley, Rich Valley, Saltville and points north, south, east and west of Saltville over the right (wrong) to own a person—slavery. The leading subject of Saltville's coveting beyond food, drink, rest, sex, religion and exercise has been athletics (which is a form of all six of the above).

I'll go heavy on athletic stories to illustrate the last quarter or final inning of this period of Shaker/Saltville history. Athletics is quite a messenger for the culture of the Valley in that era. Why athletics was such a passion in our town then and has grown to even greater force akin to religious loyalty around the nation remains a partial mystery to me. Perhaps that is the subject for another book.

My earliest "game experience" was as a nine-year-old boy riding to Marion on an unplanned trip underdressed one frigid Saturday afternoon in a breezy jeep fresh from World War II owned by Arthur and Hattie Gillenwater. Along with Mother, we witnessed the most infamous Shaker defeat in history. The 1947 football team was 9—0 going into that last game of the season, but the final score was the Scarlet Hurricanes 50 and the Shakers 0. Holy Cow! We felt like frozen and slaughtered unholy cows.

To me our finest hour covers the seasons of 1953 and 54 when the 350 plus high school enrollment from little Saltville ran up a string of victories totaling 19 over teams like Richlands, Virginia High, Marion, Abingdon and Tazewell. Equal-sized schools like Rich Valley stopped playing us then though Chilhowie and Glade Spring stayed with us for personal pride if not the big gate receipts. The scoring against schools our size was heavily Saltville even with plenty of substitutions. I remember the substitutions well because my brief playing career came only in the easy games. I'll never forget Carlous Routh coaxing assistant coach Harry Fry, later of Gate City fame, to put me in a Chilhowie game early. I got to play four quarters in a game that was ours before the opening kickoff.

They really had benches on the football sidelines then. I'll never forget those benches. We had to carry the heavy hulks from the old swimming pool to the ball park, and during games, I spent a lot of time sitting on them looking forward to getting called into action. Pine tar would ooze from the knotty lumber and combine with the green enamel to stain the seats of our pants.

I recall Coach Jeter Barker talking a Warrior Coach into scheduling a rare Friday afternoon day game at Chilhowie so we could travel that night to Abingdon to see the "biggie." Marion topped Abingdon's "James Gang" 7—6. We then beat Marion the following week 33 to 0 with only "Jesse" James' Abingdon team standing between us, the district crown and a playoff game with the Norton Raiders. Athletic logic made us a 26-point

favorite particularly since we were playing at home but
the Mighty Midgets, their official name, came to Saltville
the next week and shocked us 21—0. George F. "Jesse"
James then took Barker's place the next season. Jeter
went to Washington and Lee University just before they
de-emphasized football for academics. "Coach James"
was an awkward term of respect for those used to jeering
"Jesse." He led the Shakers to 19 victories in a row
before being topped by Johnson City's Science Hill
Hilltoppers 19—7. That school system was at least five
times our enrollment. We did not quit, and later in that
season, Saltville topped the powerful Radford Bobcats.
"Jesse" was highly successful in coaching in both Glade
Spring and Abingdon and brought a style of coaching
smart rather than coaching near brutal as was Jeter
Barker's style. In a skull (blackboard) session, our
quarterback, Alvin "Snag" Colley, great of mind and ar-
ticulation, questioned Coach James on a certain block-
ing and receivers assignment. Colley said, "Jesse, uh,
Coach, we did not do it that way last year." The short but
brusque coach replied, "It's a new regime."

For those of us who work around places that don't
want to change, it was an early insight for often in in-
stitutions we hear the seven deadly words, "We never did
it that way before." But "Snag's" variation of resistance
to change was mellowed quickly when the proud Shakers
rolled up 19 straight victories! "Jesse" James with
Saltville's Peggy Warren Harmon produced five birth
victories (children) and moved to his home territory
Wytheville to become a winner in insurance and politics.
Sadly "Jesse" died March 1992 and joined other Shaker
coaches Ray Buchanan, J. Leonard Mauck, Elmo Early,
Jeter Barker, Joe Shipley, J.C. Smith, Bill Bowman, Alex
Levicki and Alger Pugh.

Grantland Rice wrote the sports/faith finale fitting for Saltville Shaker fans in particular and U.S. Sport fans in general—"So play (live) that when that one great scorer comes to write against your name, he writes not that you've won or lost but how you played the game." Shakers Win! Holy Cow!

While athletics was a religion in Saltville, there were some great lighter times. Ralph Comer Wall, or better known as Coach "Sonny, Beans" Wall was built like a brick shipyard (or another franker Saltville phrase) before weight-lifting programs or steriods were in vogue. The bull-type physique on Sonny looked odd in a basketball game and played more oddly. Sonny would often be called for "traveling" as he would take a pass more like a backfield handoff, duck his head as a fullback and take several heavy steps toward the goal before shooting. Early in a Virginia High basketball game, we led 4 to 2, and "Beans" had scored all 6 points!

In baseball at old Shaw Stadium, Bristol, a James team (16-2) was in trouble with the Tennessee High team late in the game. "Jesse" motioned for the little lefty from McCready's Gap, Lucky "Deanie" Frye. Long before relief pitchers trotted in from the bullpen, "Deanie" did a ten-second record run from the right field bullpen. The easily angered James snorted, "Heck, Frye, just throw as hard as you run and we'll be out of this jam in three pitches."

Athletics bring funny stories but perhaps their greatest contribution centers on cultural breakthroughs. John Moore took a car load of us to Kingsport, Tennessee in 1953 to see the then New York Giants and Cleveland Indians at J. Fred Johnson Stadium, a quality class-D baseball field. The home of the Dobyns-Bennett football and baseball Indians was the biggest park we

tenth graders had seen. It was also the largest number
of black folk we had ever encountered. During the
days of public segregation, we saw the entire right-field
bank of bleachers relegated to blacks, perhaps as many
as a thousand. Possibly because two of the most black-
populated teams were New York and Cleveland, the
small number of blacks in east Tennessee turned out in
great numbers. That day we saw negroes (we struggled
to pronounce that word correctly) Willie Mays, Larry
Doby, Luke Easter, Monty Irvin, and Hank Thomson
mix with whites like Early Wynn, hispanic Mike Garcia,
Bob Feller, Bob Lemon, Alvin Dark and Bobby Thomson. I wondered how the races could mix completely on
the field and get along but the law then read we must sit
separately and equally. But of course the right-field foul-
line seats are not exactly equal.

Thirty-eight years later, I watched a Dobyns-Bennett
High School game of football on the same field and was
moved in a special way when a black back for the Indians, Lamont Jones, returned a Volunteer High kickoff
for 91 yards on the opening play as several thousand of
Kingsport's finest black and white fans equally dispersed
in good seating roared raw approval. Time and whatever
else make a difference even in the same setting.

Athletics in and beyond Saltville may have helped us
with race relations better than religion and status bar-
riers. Wags said then and have been proved rather
right—the last places to be integrated will be the country
clubs and churches.

A key presence for a lively Shaker football game was
the lively Shaker band. Indeed, Saltville had one lively
band, led in those days by Minnesota transplant Luroy
C. Krumwiede who was far from a southern Saltville red
neck. His conflicts with Coach Jeter Barker were many

and mammoth. But the Shaker High School Band, 48 strong (which had to recruit down to the fifth grade) fared well in concert and marching form. From polished pieces like "In a Persian Market Place" to John Philip Sousa's prancy pieces, we loved the Shaker Band's songs. Tradition was to play the school song "Our Director" after each touchdown. The alumni and student stood and sang, "Three cheers for Saltville High School, Maroon and Gray, Cheers for our Colors, They will never fade. We pledge to be of service until we die. We will support our dear Saltville High."

The most graphic scene I recall was the day one half of our brand new band uniforms arrived for the big homecoming parade fifteen minutes shy of the 4 p.m. parade start time. Our Police Chief, Branham, flew the town cruiser from the Tri-Cities Airport to the high school basement and hurriedly dragged two monstrous boxes of new band uniforms across the old concrete floor. As he passed the cafeteria (some dubbed the Rachel Catron Memorial Cafeteria) on his way to the cramped band room No. 13, forty-eight happy Shaker band members (as Jeter Barker was wont to call them, "piccolo players") stood in two flanking lines between the old steps to the gym/auditorium and the band room and roared their approval. For some reason, I recall a majorette sash trailing outside one of the boxes and tripping up the good police chief as he alternately dragged and dirtied the sash with his big feet. But come time for the 4 p.m. plant whistle blast and the parade start, Chief Branham's lovely and lanky daughter June Branham DeBord blew her whistle, and all 48 band members were in place and stepping high in our stately military type Shaker maroon and gray uniforms—direct from Wilkes-Barre, Pennsylvania via Chief Branham and the Tri-Cities Airport. We rolled the drums, "Mert" gave the blast, and we played as never before, "Three cheers for Saltville High School." Holy Cow! Luroy and Jeter notwithstanding.

Chapter 11

Big A, Notchie and Morgan Farm

Eugene "Notchie" Cregger, a brother to our Easy Street Neighbor Jim Cregger, triggers a string of Cregger stories though not in categories.

"Notchie" sought special spiritual direction one Tuesday night and attended the Main Street Christian Church's prayer meeting conducted by Mrs. Will Brickey. The sessions seemed helpful to the usual corporal's guard present. So Mrs. Brickey had the faithful circle agree to say a sentence prayer. Jack Catron thanked God for music, Claude Smith for revival, and Harold Puckett for food. Now by counterclock rotation came "Notchie's" turn. After a protracted silence, the leader awkwardly said, "Mr. Cregger, it's your turn to pray." Eugene "Notchie" replied in poker parlance, "I pass." Church and prayer meeting were out!

"Notchie" also loved baseball as did his son-in-law E. Roy "Buck" Arnold, Jr. Being a great Yankee fan, Buck decided to give his father-in-law a big trip to Washington, D.C., for a Senators-Yankee series.

Many stories abounded on their return including "Notchie's" dismay that none of the D.C. restaurants served raw onions. Whereupon Mr. Cregger started

brown bagging that Vidalia forerunner and cere-
moniously carved a big onion with his pocket knife
during salad time as "Buck" and others took embarrassed shelter in the nearby restrooms.

Most notably remembered by "Notchie" was "Buck's"
bragging about Mickey Mantle's long ball hitting ability.
In one of Mantle's rare batting strategies, the "Mick"
bunted for a scratch hit. "Notchie" was not impressed.
When asked about the longest trip Eugene "Notchie"
had ever taken, he always led, "Why, I went all the way to
Washington, D.C., with my son-in-law "Buck" Arnold.
Why we went to see the mighty Yankees and the great
homerun hitter Mickey Mantle. Yes, I went all the way to
Washington to see Mickey Mantle and he blunted!"

"Notchie's" older brother Jim was quieter and less
descriptive, but his wife Mabel Cumbo Cregger was
among Easy Street's most colorful characters. She was
the typical stay-at-home wife/mother of the 1940s and
'50s. Jim and Mabel had six healthy well-educated
children.

One of my saddest declines for funeral requests had
to go to the Cregger family when they requested my
burying both of their parents. Distance and previous pastoral commitments prohibited.

Mabel had a large wart on the right tip of her tongue.
It was a curiosity to us kids who would stare at it and
were surprised at her ability to talk long, loud and swiftly, but she never seemed to catch or bite that huge wart.

My biggest disappointment with Mrs. Cregger centered on our miscommunication. She kept a cow in their
backyard barn, and grazed it in the pasture field which
is now the high school campus. On occasion, she would
entice the neighborhood kids to "drive" old Betsy back
to the pasture. One particularly cold day, she caught me
and promised me a nice brownie if I would oblige. I

took the cow to pasture and rushed back to her back door expecting a hot tasty baked brownie. She gave me a new shiny penny!

Mother laughed about Mabel's descriptive terms for the vertical malfunction so common in the original black and white TVs. The Creggers were the first to have a TV on the Easy Street hill. One night as mother and Mabel were watching Amos 'n Andy, the problem started and Mabel summoned her husband, "Lord God, Jim, get in here. This TV set is turning somersaults."

The topper of the Cregger stories came during that day when neighbors borrowed often and anything from neighbors: a cup of sugar or coffee, a wrench, a wheelbarrow, or whatever would be borrowed and loaned without much question. Mrs. Cregger had a heavily adorned wrap around front porch banister with every variety of flowers and running plants streaming every which way. Mother slipped over rather sheepishly to borrow a sanitary napkin. She requested the product quietly because of the close proximity of three front porches laden with friendly but curious neighbors. Mother whispered, "Mrs. Cregger, do you have a sanitary napkin I can borrow?" Mabel responded resoundly, "Lord no, Ruth, I ain't got no Kotex, but I've got a gardenia with a root on it."

Mabel Cregger was funny and fun but not well-known because of her staying close to home.

Perhaps Saltville's best known and beloved commoner citizen was Aaron Allison, affectionately called "Big A." Aaron had a fall in childhood which did brain damage. His energetic, friendly and sometimes abrupt manner was soon learned and always loved by others. The nickname came on the first day of school. He was asked to spell his first name. Since he was not pronouncing Aaron clearly, the teacher persisted in calling on him to repeat his name. Bothered by the embarrassment, he said in anger, "A...A...r...o...n, big 'a' little 'a'...'r'... 'o'...'n,' and then gave out one of his trademark belches which rattled George Washington's picture in the near-by hallway of Allison Gap School. Thus, his nickname was ever in the Saltville tradition "Big A."

Aaron loved watches and clocks. He would display over a dozen wrist watches on either arm at the same time. He also carried large piggy banks around and people would stuff money in them though I never saw "Big A" bum money. He did have a falling out with the *Saltville Progress* newspaper over money. The paper allowed him to carry extra copies of their weekly around town. It was O.K. by them for "Big A" to keep whatever money he collected. But "Big A" then began to empty out the coin boxes from the paper's newsstand containers and pocket that money also. He never understood the paper's logic, and when corrected, got mad and quit all sales.

Perhaps many a Saltville native picked up "A's" habit of stopping at every day phone in Saltville to check for the forgotten dime. To this day I often check phones especially since the 25 cent call. Once at the Chicago O'-Hare Airport with a row of 25 phones, I earned $3.75.

My most embarrassing moment came as I was observed (caught) checking three phones at the Earlanger Hospital in Chattanooga, Tennessee, by one of our church member doctors. I got a good raise the next year but I still check pay phones when I can. It is amazing how much fewer quarters are forgotten now than dimes after the cost of local calls went up 150 percent. And if we do not think our habits are considered by our children, I notice our daughters Jean and Carla checking out coin slots in public telephones.

Jerry Willis submitted one of the two best known "Big A" stories. Aaron was supported by relatives since government and schools took little interest in special education during his formative years. He was always well if not oddly dressed (a hippy forerunner in wide ties and outlandish color and fabric combinations). "A" was always clean and looked well fed. In his latter years, Henderson Flower Shop supplied "A" with a carnation which he personally delivered to the funeral home for placement near the coffin at every Saltville death. It was simply signed "Big A." Willis also reports the often quoted Allison philosophy, "The people in the Gap (Allison) and Saltville think I'm crazy because I don't work. I don't work, have plenty, go where and when I want to, got plenty of friends and very few worries. Why, I think they're the ones who are crazy for working too hard and worrying too much."

Coach Sonny "Beans" Wall of Danville, Virginia, assures us of not missing the other oft circulated Allison jewel. It seems Police Chief Charlie Norris rushed into Mrs. Cuddy's restaurant for a quick cup of coffee before driving to Marion for a court case. "Big A" was relaxed as usual, chatting and drinking coffee. Charlie sat down beside and jumped a little as he tasted his fresh cup of coffee, "It's too damn hot, 'Big A,'" Charlie quipped. "Big A" simply pulled Charlie's cup over to his place and scooted his cup over to the chief and said, "Take mine, Charlie, it's done been saucered and blowed."

Charlie Starks, pastor of the Broadford United Methodist Church Circuit, recalls "Big A" was walking across the main intersection of Saltville one Sunday morning carrying a huge pulpit type Bible. Herb Davidson asked "A" where he was going with that big Bible. Aaron replied, a bit irritated, "Why, to church, Herb."

"Well, Big A, why are you carrying that big Bible. Everybody knows you can't read." "A" kept walking and replied again in a peaceful confidence to Herb, who might have been his only critic, "No, I can't read, but I can sure show whose side I'm on."

On October 3, 1987, Aaron "Big A" Allison was buried in the Elizabeth Cemetery. There were many folk and flowers and we all knew whose side "A" was on in this life and which side of the stormy Jordan banks contains his forwarding address—belches and all.

Entertainment for teenagers and others in the Saltville fifties was limited with stereos and rock music. TV involved one snowy station from WJHL originally and stock car racing was infant. Some of the clan once drove to the District of Columbia to see the dominant Cleveland Browns and the weak Redskins with football tickets easier to get there than girlie show tickets. There was only one professional football team televised in our area then with WCYB Bristol having a weekly contract with Paul and Jimmy Brown's Cleveland Browns.

One Christmas season a group of us boys in our late high school years started walking around the town observing the home Christmas decorations. The colorful electric lights were a welcomed relief to the dark cold December weather of Saltville. One of us decided it would be cute, adventurous and risky to slip up quietly on the decorated doors and outside trees and twist loose some bulbs causing the owner to wonder what happened. We would then watch at a safe distance until the owner would start switching on and off his control switch but to no avail. On certain older light systems, it took only one loosened bulb to turn the entire circuit dark.

However, George Heimann failed to get the procedure down. He thought we were pocketing the bulbs. He had on a long overcoat with deep pockets. I finally heard the glassy grating of dozens of bulbs from George's pocket as he awkwardly gaited across Paul Price's front yard. Our dilemma was how to return so many and so varied a collection of Christmas tree lights from George's deep pockets. About the time we decided to huddle for a return of bulbs strategy, Joe Dab Moore's mother Blanche interdicted us roadside near Fon Cook's. She stopped the old 1940 Chevrolet truck and bid us aboard. She assured us the police force was out in force looking for Christmas light thieves. She and other mothers shamed our creative game not much believing that George had misunderstood the light to dark approach. The only solution that would get us back in Blanche's graces was immediate group front-porch apologies and an even more embarrassing and awkward return of the stolen bulbs with the awful question, "Do any of these look like your bulbs?" I did get Blanche to let us skip Mabel Clear's house since George had burned his hand on a big blue bulb there and ran away squawking and I had Mabel as my algebra I teacher and was in enough grade trouble as it was.

Later we marveled at the forgiveness granted our apologies but wondered who figured out our identity (Stan McCready, Joe Dab Moore, Brack Morgan, Don Smith, and George Heimann) since we staged each hit most anonymously. People and patterns were so well-known with a small town population that we finally found out Blanche was talking by phone to Mary Sue Totten when we hit K.O. "Pie" Totten's place. The immediate darkness got the always observant hospital reception-nurse's attention. She slipped to her front door and saw only a single foot of us eight fleeing pranksters. But as incredible as it is, she recognized Joe Dab Moore's foot as he jumped off her porch. She then said, "Blanche, I know Joe is involved. I recognized his foot."

The earliest law enforcers I knew were Chief Branham and Lambert, town policemen. I remember Uncle Charlie DeBusk as a Smyth County plain-clothes deputy because he carried a hidden holster revolver and had a small badge pinned to the back side of his wide tie which swung down dangling as he dipped ice cream from the old two-gallon cardboard container at the drug store he operated.

"Jingo" Lambert, who eventually became chief of the Saltville police force, was by far the most verbally abused. Many embarrassing and humorous stories about "Jingo" were circulated throughout the area. We knew the Lamberts as neighbors. The west end of Saltville visited at will their admission free, no-hours backyard zoo. From the gold fish pond to the monkey cage, we simply let ourselves in and out, careful not to let loose any of the quaint members of the Lambert zoo.

Jingo locked people up for a living but few required that extreme and I know no stories from the lockups. The first story may be apocryphal since I've heard it on other community law enforcers. But the latter two are vintage Saltville/Lambert and with that given, our once esteemed zoo keeper and less esteemed police chief may have done all three.

An Ohio transplant came to Mathieson to work one December. By June he was still displaying Ohio car tags quite noticeable to all of us in the 1940s. Officer Lambert finally decided to challenge the man's violation of the law. He innocently asked, "Where are you from, man?" The transplant said, "Cincinnati." The locally trained policeman replied in incredible detective like tones, "By gollies, then what are you doing with those Ohio tags on?"

The second story occurred before the days of Highway 107 the most direct route between Saltville and county seat Marion was a road with several key turns that included the almost perfect replica of a horseshoe around the steep mountain. It was well known as "Horseshoe Bend." The best connecting road to the Marion route from downtown Saltville was a road between the well fields and the golf course which wound up a series of steep curves called the Pike. Car shoppers used to test drive straight shift cars up the Pike. If the car could pull the Pike in no more than second gear, it passed.

One night, a stranger to Smyth County stopped our chief for directions from downtown Saltville to Marion. After much thought the stately looking town official said, "All right, son, you take the Pike to the top, keep going 'til you hit the Morgan farm, then bear right at the Morgan farm and keep going and you're there." A stranger to all these local terms was confused especially at not knowing which farm would be the Morgan farm. Lambert, in total disbelief, started on his way home, looked back over his shoulder at the stranger and said, "Aye Gollies, son, if you don't know where the Morgan farm is, I don't know how to tell you to get to Marion."

The third faux pas may show more grace than ignorance. "Jingo" was patrolling a lover's lane and discovered a parked car. He stuck his flashlight and head into the window of the car discovering a boy and a girl amorously entangled. In his characteristically intoned and inquiring voice, he exclaimed, "What are you all doing in there?" The resourceful boy countered, "Why,

Mr. Lambert, we're just sitting out here watching the moon." The always trusting and always doubting chief retrieved his flashlight and head from the car window and searched the heavily clouded skies. Then he said, "Aye Gollies, folks, I think you'd better get your clothes back on and get out of here before somebody catches you." As he walked toward his car, he was overheard to say, "The dumb kids, there ain't no moon out here tonight."

Frank "Ob" Cox reported a Saltville girl was found walking late one night alone and upset. As she shared her story, her fear and anger turned to amusement. We would call her story a sexual harassment encounter today. It seems that one of Saltville's more sexually determined but scared boys had taken her far out to a deserted parking place. He had meant to use the old cliche, "Put out or get out." Having no desire to oblige his real intentions, the young woman had started walking home when the police stopped to help. Ob asked, "What did he say to you to make you walk this far?" She smiled and mocked his stuttering style. He said, "Get...get...g...g...get...o...o...get out...Get out or go...go...or go home...Get out or go home"!

This story is from John "Beans" Wall of Atlanta, Georgia. John writes:

> My Saltville story is about greed on my part and knowledge and foresight on Joe Vernon's part. During most of World War II, I worked for Joe Vernon at his barber shop with duties that involved arriving at 7 a.m., building a fire in his coal burning stove to heat up the water and the shop. I also kept the shop clean and was the shoe shining boy. I would shine shoes until 8:30 a.m. and then

go to school. I would return after school and work until the shop closed. Believe it or not, I made myself $12 to $15 per week and that was good money for someone twelve or thirteen years old at that time. After I had been there for some time, I got the bright idea that I would quit school and shine shoes full time. This way I felt I could make a lot more money. I told Joe Vernon my plans and he told me that he would talk with me after the shop closed that night. When the shop closed, Joe informed me that if I quit school I no longer had a job at his barber shop. Also he said if I quit school, he would wear out his razor strap on my bottom. I never did entertain the thought of quitting school again. I have always appreciated what Joe did for me. Thanks Joe, wherever you are.

John Wall, the original "Beans"

P.S.: I still love beans and could easily eat them everyday and usually do.

This letter is from a well-known Saltville teacher:

My memories of Saltville and the people would fill a book with two parts. There were the first years, 1940 to 1941. At that time, I doubt if you could find a more desirable place to teach.

You might enjoy this little story about Edna Price who proved to J. Leonard Mauck that you don't have to be tall to play basketball. With Edna as our star, we took a woman's basketball team to Roanoke to play basketball with the National Business College. We were badly beaten and Edna, who was so accurate with her basketball shots, was shooting for the rim. "Edna," we asked, "why were you shooting for the rim?" Her very surprising answer was, "They said the backboards were made of glass, and I was afraid I might break them."

I remember a remark J. Leonard Mauck made one time that was typical of him. He said, "When I have to punish a student, I always go out of my way to pick him up in my car or do something nice for him so he will know that I didn't think less of him." I have so many memories of your family and the Arnold boys and all the boys and teachers and principals who were part of my years in Saltville. Maybe I should get my typewriter back from my friend and start the book.

Audry Harden
(Retired as librarian in 1968 and resides in
Abingdon, Virginia)

Another story submitted by a Saltville resident:

During World War II Madam Russell Methodist Church mailed all of its members who were in the armed forces a New Testament and a little book titled *Strength for Service to God and Country.*

I carried these two books with me throughout the war and still have them. They were with me when I crossed the North Atlantic in a large convoy through U-boat infested waters. They were with me during the air raids on London. They were with me during the buzz-bomb raids at Portsmouth, England. They were with me when I crossed the English Channel on an LST and landed at Omaha Beach in Normandy. They were with me when I crossed France. They were with me during the Battle of the Bulge. They were with me when I went across the Seigfried

Line and into Germany. They were with me when VE Day came. They came back home with me and I have had these two books now for fifty years. The sad part of the story is that I scarcely read the books. They were tucked away in my duffle bag. I spent all my spare time drinking beer and wine and fraternizing with the European women. Looking back—it was a very sinful life indeed and one that I am very ashamed of having done the things that I did. But now after having given my life to God, the books are no longer tucked away in a duffle bag, but are being read daily. Yes, the books and I went through a lot of bad times but God looked out for us and took care of us, and I am so thankful that before the last chapter of Buck Arnold's life is over, God gave me another chance to make things right. And like the books which were always with me, I now realize that God was always with me. Thank God, I finally, before it was too late, gave my life to Him...

...So long for now. Keep up the good work. Regards to all and pray for me. I am keeping up the good fight.

Your friend, Buck
(Buck Arnold resides in the
Poor Valley section of Saltville.)

Dr. E.E. "Ned" Wiley, United Methodist Historian and premier pulpiteer, had Saltville ties both as the Abingdon District Superintendent of the Holston Conference covering United Methodist Churches surrounding Saltville, Quarry, Plasterco, and Manaheim as well as Madam Russell United Methodist Church.

I was enamored with his preaching at the old Saltville High School auditorium/gymnasium for sister Mabel June "Whizzie's" baccalaureate or class sermon as they called it in the spring of 1951. Ned, a short man, danced in an agile way as he rolled off the Greek alphabet poetry and a powerful sermon. I wondered then as I still wonder today, "What would churches be like if we could get strong people like Ned into the pulpit?"

He also caused us to roar in laughter (not common in sermons then) when he compared the Virginia and Tennessee sections of the Holston Conference. The Chattanooga native said, "When you're sent to Virginia, they give the preacher three bedrooms and a bath. In Tennessee, you get three bedrooms and a path." Ned and Frances were never as well known in Saltville as they were in Bristol, Kingsport, Chattanooga and Newport, but Ned was always supportive of me and this book. Thanks, Wileys

A story from Ned:

> I remember my father's half-brother Charlie Wiley (who stuttered) and Cousin Jenny and their family. Their son, Dr. William Wiley, lived with his family in Kingsport when I was pastor of Broad Street Methodist Church on the church circle. At Christmas the four churches on the circle would assemble, each on its steps at night and sing a Christmas carol. Then we would all go down to the church circle Christmas tree at the center of the circle and sing, "Joy to the World, the Lord is come."
>
> One Sunday morning at 6:45 a.m., cousin Jenny Wiley (visiting her son William) passed the Broad Street parsonage walking down to the

Roman Catholic church a few blocks away. I was out sweeping our walk. "Good morning, cousin Ned, why don't you join me for mass at my church this morning?" said cousin Jenny. "I'll be glad to, cousin Jenny, if you will come with me afterwards and worship at Broad Street Methodist Church," I replied. "Sorry, but I can't do that, cousin Ned," she commented ruefully. Later, I gave Dr. William Wiley the vows of membership in the Broad Street Church.

French Taylor pastored Madam Russell United Methodist Church from 1946 to 1952. The short of stature and tall on faith fellow shocked some conservative religious folk by smoking and frequenting the community pool hall called "The Rat Hole." (Because of its dark, damp basement sitting under the drug store next to the Victory Theater.) His gracious widow Laverta of Knoxville, Tennessee, was able at growing and arranging flowers as well as lifting and helping folk share these stories. French died in 1990.

French's stories:

A Cure for Rheumatism

The hospital in Saltville in the early days of my ministry was located upstairs over the Mathieson Company General Store—a drug store, general merchandise, and grocery store. There was a long flight of steps leading from the street level to the hospital and the doctor's offices.

I was on my way up those steps to visit a member of my congregation when Dr. McKee came out the door and started down the steps. A man on his way up to see the Doctor called out, "Dr. McKee, are you leaving? I want you to do something about this rheumatism of mine. It's killing me!" Dr. McKee held out his cane to the gentleman and replied, "Here, take this cane and I'll get another one. If I could do anything about rheumatism, I would do it for myself!"

The Episcopal Church:
Are they of the high or low order?

The Madam Russell Church in Saltville was my first appointment after returning from Guam in the South Pacific where I served as a chaplain in the Air Force during World War II.

I arrived in Saltville late in the evening thrilled to be back home with my family and eager to get on with the challenges of the new pastorate. I parked our car and trailer full of our belongings in front of the parsonage. The parsonage at the time was a large two story frame house next to the church in the downtown area.

A man leaning against the fence that surrounded the parsonage and church seemed eager to talk with this stranger who had just arrived in town. In the conversation, I asked about the churches in Saltville. With a limited knowledge of church life, he hesitated and then replied, "Down the street a little way is the Episcopal Church." Knowing that various forms of order and ceremony are permitted in the American Episcopal Church, I inquired, "Is it the high or the low Episcopal Church?" Again, he hesitated for a moment and replied, "Some of them get pretty high!"

Arthur Phillips pastor of Madam Russell Church from 1963 to 1966 was a scholar. He asked me to write the introduction for his book, *Stories in Categories*. I hope he doesn't haunt me for placing his story in the catch-all chapter. The Phillips are both in Heaven and left two sons who are United Methodist ministers. Arthur advised me not to go to seminary in 1966. He said it might ruin me. Perhaps he was right! I went.

This is Arthur's story:

> Three sisters living out in the country near Saltville wanted to get married in the Madam Russell Church. They asked me how much it would cost to use the church. I told them there would be no charge for the use of the church but the groom usually gave the custodian $2.00 for cleaning the church after the wedding. I performed a joint ceremony for the three sisters. The custodian was handed $6.00 and I was given $3.00.

Jim McCready (no kin) "ran" the bank in Saltville for many years. I came to know him and his gracious wife Jo (deceased in 1992) as a rookie minister at Byars Cobb United Methodist Church in Glade Spring where he was the treasurer. He commuted the nine miles to Saltville (it seemed a long distance then); and in order to start his car on cold mornings, he placed a simple 100 watt light bulb next to the engine block and, "She turned over on the first try each morning."

Jim shares the story of "Fon" Cook, a well-known enterpriser in the Saltville '40s:

> "Notchie" Cregger came into the bank and asked Clyde Crafts, bank president, for a hundred dollar loan. Clyde told him he would need a good endorser and suggested that "Notchie" go out and

get "Fon" Cook to sign the note and he could get the money. "Notchie" took the bank note to "Fon" and requested his signature so that he could get the money. "Fon" said, "You go and get Clyde to endorse it, and I will give you the loan!"

Ron Coulthard submitted this story:

A bunch of neighborhood teenagers, "Nyoka" Cannon, "Dab" Moore, the Price brothers and I used to gather at the home of a Saltvillian who is now a prominent minister. Once I had in my possession a special kind of telescope. You could look into this apparatus and by turning a dial, view a series of very healthy nude women. We were passing this around when the future minister came up with an ingenious idea. He got the family film projector by telling his mother that we wanted to watch some old home movies. We went into the basement, put up a sheet for a screen, then broke open the peep show telescope and fed the film into the projector. It worked great! We were whooping it up at the now life size beauties when our host mother opened the basement door, snapped on the light and said, "I made you boys some brownies." When she saw what we were doing, she didn't exactly take the Lord's name in vain, but as I recall she did exclaim, "Home movies, my a...!"

Submitted by Ron Coulthard and totally forgotten by the aforementioned minister. Ron is an English professor at Appalachian State University and has published a book on grammar.

Gladys Patton Davidson, Asbury Acres, Maryville, Tennessee, being of sound Saltville mind must report these memories:

I'm ready to start hollering down the rain barrel so the nurses say! However, I have one sin yet to commit. I've got to take to drinking Sanka.

The Mathieson Alkali in Saltville, Smyth County, Virginia, subsidized everything in the town of about a thousand people. Saltville was the home of two Revolutionary War Generals. They were both husbands of Madam Russell (at separate times, of course). The Madam Russell Methodist Church was named for Madam Russell. It was a Union Church. I wish I could go back to the church there. I remember the tiny chairs we sat in in the primary Sunday school class. (I would have to just look now. There's no way I could sit in one!) The first minister I remember was Reverend Wingo. Stan's grandfather was a kindly generous man. He was so generous that he took all the children of the neighborhood for a ride when he bought the first Buick in the county. My father owned an Oakland automobile! But I felt "big" riding in a Buick! Mr. and Mrs. McCready had two boys and two girls at that time. We all played together in the back yard at the McCreadys. That's all there was to do in Saltville.

One day Mrs. McCready needed some groceries. She sent Wesley King (we called him "Dad") to the store. Dad returned from the store and we all sat down in the back yard to eat the ice cream Dad had brought along with the groceries.

Just as everyone was blissfully beginning to eat, Mrs. McCready came to the door and said, "Dad, I forgot to tell you to get soda. Please dash back for it. I need it now to make the biscuits." "Dad" regarded each of us for a moment as he was afraid we would eat his ice cream. So he said aloud, "I'll just stick my big toe in the bowl of cream to assure that no one else eats my ice cream." And he proceeded to do just that. I'm certain that his toe needed washing as we all went barefooted from May 10 to the first frost.

While we were courting, Perry, my husband, took me to the Alkalite (it was a picture show not a chemical) to a matinee. He swears that two dogs chased each other up and down the aisle before deciding to have a scrap on the stage.

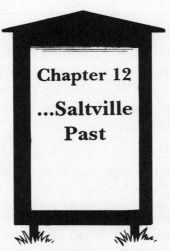

You Are the Salt of the Earth

From multiple viewings at theatres "Victory" and "Salt" to Atlanta's "Fox" my favorite movie is Margaret Mitchell's "Gone with the Wind".

The shy southern sister's only book once served as couch leg substitute in its original manuscript for several years. She refused a New York Publisher's offer during a personal visit only to change her mind and chase him down at the train station with her now world famous manuscript in hand. How eerie to think "what might NOT have been from her words and pen."

Her story of the ole south is best summed up in the movie prologue:

> *There was a land of cavaliers and cotton*
> *fields called the old South.*
> *Here in the patrician world, the age of*
> *chivalry took its last bow...*
> *Here was the last ever to be seen of*
> *knights and their ladies fair...of*
> *master and slave...*
> *Look for it only in books, for it is no*
> *more than a dream remembered, a*
> *civilization gone with the wind.*

The National Archives Building in Washington, D.C. bears these frontal words from its majestic columns "The Past Is Prologue". Combining the fictional world of Keelor's Wobegon and Mitchell's Tarra brings us to a curious and candid conclusion.

We are yet alive and see each others face. And the faces of our past through our memories and their faith in each of us and a holy God.

Sister Mitchell's era was "gone" with the wind of a single crop economy (cotton) and an evil much worse than the bole weevil—human slavery. Spiritual progress did "overcome" that day.

But the era of 1945 to 1965 in Saltville and other places like her, need not bow out by "blowing in the wind", as said in songs of the sixties.

The ten basic commandments of our Creator, God are as valid for us today as they were at Sinai 4,000 years ago or in Saltville 200 years ago. There is no process under Heaven through which the "big ten" can be repealed. They are commands not suggestions or options.

So in a day when standards stagger and mistrust mushrooms, we conclude for now with a light tongue in cheek song written about me and Saltville and a serious tongue in soul revisit of the Gettysburg Address.

The Holy City (Saltville)

I was passing by a church house and decided to go in. Saw a man there at the altar, introduced myself to him. He said, "Son I am the preacher, come and rest your weary head. I said, "Preacher, where do you come from?" And this is what he said:

Chorus 1
He said, "I'm from the Holy City nestled in the rollin' hills. There's no place like that Holy City, the one they call Saltville."
Oh I listened as he told me of that city over there. When he finished all his stories we both had a word of prayer. I departed on my journey, his words ringing in my ears. My life has a new direction, and the way now seems so clear.

Chorus 2
I want to see that Holy City, I'm gonna start my journey now. When I get to that Holy City, I'll milk those holy cows.
I want to see that Holy City, and if I live I know I will. I've heard about that Holy City, the one they call Saltville.

> Copyrighted by
> Ken Alfrey, 1992
> Mafair United Methodist Church
> Kingsport, TN
> Written for a church fellowship program.

Saltville and Gettysburg

Maggie Moore required her seventh grade classes and I my eleventh grade classes to recite publicly Lincoln's classic 272 word address now in marble in his D.C. Memorial. Little did I realize then how well his outline can highlight our "civil wars" of this day.

Twelve score and four years ago our fore fathers and mothers brought forth in this crop and chemical rich valley a new town conceived in work and family and dedicated to the proposition that all Shakers and others are equal.

Now we are engaged in a great spiritual and social war, testing whether that town or any church so conceived and so dedicated can truly endure. We meet daily on great battle fields of these wars.

We come regularly in worship and work to dedicate a portion of our fields of dreams. We honor their final resting place, Elizabeth Cemetery (named after Madam Elizabeth Russell) and other sacred burial places, those who gave their last full measure of devotion that a people might live better. It is altogether fitting and proper that we should do this. But in a greater sense, Mr. Lincoln, Mr. Worthy, Mrs. Moore and Dr. McKee have already done this far above our poor power to add or detract.

The world will little note nor long remember Saltville.

But it is for us the living rather to be dedicated to all great tasks remaining before us that from these honored dead we take increased devotion. That we now highly restore that these dead shall not have died in vain.

That Saltville, under God, shall have a new birth and that life in this valley shall be of God's people, by God and His Commands and for all God's people and then God's ways and people shall not perish from God's good earth.

"You are the salt of the earth."
Matthew 5:13
63 A.D.
The Shakers (do) play better in the rain.
by Stan McCready
A.D. 1992

Additional Copies of "The Shakers Play Better in the Rain" may be ordered from:

McCready Ministries
1409 East Center St.
Kingsport, TN 37664